Every Rose

TAKE A CHANCE, BOOK 4

Nancy Warren

AMBLESIDE PUBLISHING

Every Rose
Take a Chance Book 4
Copyright © 2015 Nancy Weatherley Warren

Discover other titles by Nancy Warren at
www.NancyWarren.net

One

MIND OVER MATTER, Rose Chance muttered to herself as she strode across the linoleum floor of Portland's Pacific Crest hospital. She'd known in the shoe store that the Prada heels weren't comfortable, but when she looked at herself in the mirror and admired the black and red pump with the ice pick heels, she decided they were comfy enough.

That was before she'd put in a twelve-hour day. She needed a large, chilled glass of white wine, a blister bandage and her feet up. Instead, she still had to check on her patient. Who knew Belinda Tate would birth three babies who all arrived ahead of schedule and that number four would be a dawdler? Which meant that instead of an easy day in the office breaking in her new shoes, she was going to be on her pretty but aching feet for some hours yet waiting for little Tate number four.

When she entered the birthing suite she paused just inside the door. Before she inserted herself into nature's birthing process she liked to stand on the outside and watch the laboring mother, the interaction between her and her husband or partner or whatever helpers she brought in with her. She liked to see firsthand the relationship developing between the patient and the nurses assigned to her. Rose had helped birth enough babies to understand that during these crucial hours, mothers-to-be developed an important bond with the nurses who stayed with them and helped them through the process.

Belinda Tate was already a mother of three, so she knew the drill. Her husband, Charlie, sat on a chair by her bedside, holding her hand. Her other hand rested on the enormous mound of her belly. Anita, the nurse in charge of the patient, was refilling Belinda's plastic water glass. She murmured something Rose couldn't hear and Belinda laughed. This birthing team was a good one. Rose stepped inside the room. "How's it going?"

Belinda glanced up and gave her a tired smile. "However many times you do this, it never gets easier." She shifted her back against the pillows. "I was saying to Charlie that this is it for me. As soon as I get home, we're scheduling him that vasectomy."

Charlie jerked his hips back at her words, jamming his butt against the plastic chair. He was a big bear of a man, with shaggy hair and the kind of plaid shirt that passes for high fashion in Portland. "Now honey, you know you should never make big decisions when you're in labor." Rose couldn't tell whether he really wanted more children or whether he was afraid of the vasectomy, but she agreed that this wasn't the time for that discussion.

She wondered that anyone had four kids. After

growing up in the noise and chaos of a household containing eleven children she had long ago decided she was never having kids. After assisting in nearly a hundred births and then treating the babies as they suffered through everything from ear infections to broken bones, she wondered why any woman ever had more than one child. She was an excellent doctor, however, and kids really took to her, so no one knew her true feelings. Well, she was fairly certain a couple of her siblings were on to her. They probably shared her horror of the chaos of their childhood.

"Do you mind if I examine you now?"

"How about after this contraction," Belinda gasped. She grabbed the bed rail with one hand and tightened her grip on her husband's hand with the other. She leaned forward, grunting.

"That's right honey, you're doing great," Charlie said, rubbing his wife's shoulder with his free hand.

Rose lifted her wrist and counted the time on the Cartier watch her last lover had bestowed on her while they enjoyed a skiing trip in the Alps. The watch had already outlasted him by a year and she suspected it would still be keeping perfect time long after she'd forgotten Jonathan's name.

When Belinda fell back, sweat gleaming on her forehead, Rose calculated that the contraction had lasted fifty seconds. She turned to Anita. "How far apart are they?"

"Between three and five minutes. Not regular."

She pulled on a pair of surgical gloves and settled herself on the stool at the bottom of the birthing bed. "Okay, let's take a look."

A quick examination indicated that things were progressing normally. "You're almost 7 cm dilated. She peeled off the gloves, replaced the privacy sheet and patted Belinda on the knee. "I'm sure I don't need to tell you to try walking around, keep pushing that water, and try to relax as much as you can between contractions."

"I will. Thanks, Rose."

She conferred with Anita for a few minutes. In her thirty-year career, Anita had helped bring hundreds, if not thousands of babies into the world, and the nurse agreed with her initial assessment that they were several hours away from the birth.

She double-checked that Anita had her pager number and then decided to head down to the doctors' lounge where she could grab a cold bottle of water and catch up on some paperwork. She contemplated running home to her condo to change her shoes, but, even though she only lived fifteen minutes away from the hospital, babies were far too unpredictable for her to take the risk.

* * *

DR. MATTIUS VASILOPOLOUS pulled his shoulder blades together, trying to ease the kink in his upper back. Four hours bent over a surgery table was hell on the spine. He reached the waiting room where the young wife of his latest patient sat, staring into space, an open magazine on her lap, an untouched cup of coffee from the machine beside her on the table. Her eyes were red rimmed and her posture was brittle.

When she caught sight of him her body seemed to stiffen even more, as though she were steeling herself for bad news. Thank God he didn't have to deliver heartbreak. Not tonight. The thoracic aortic aneurism repair he'd done on her husband was a success.

He didn't waste a second leaving her in suspense. "Melanie, right?"

"Yes." She nodded. Got to her feet stiffly, the magazine tumbling to the ground. "My husband…?"

"He's stable."

"Oh, thank God." She put a hand to her mouth.

He spoke again, because he never, ever gave false hope. "We were able to stop the bleeding and we've fixed the weak spot in his aorta with a graft, but he's going to have to go on blood pressure medication, and he's smoked his last cigarette."

She nodded, weeping quietly. "When can I see him?"

"You can go in now for a few minutes." The guy was out cold but Matt understood that loved ones who'd been afraid of the worst needed to see that their person was breathing before they could believe that they were going to live.

When he'd handed her off to a nurse, he headed for the doctors' lounge. He needed a shower, he needed food, and he needed sleep.

If there was one thing he'd learned as a cardio-thoracic surgeon it was how to get by on snatched naps. The irony was that, as a doctor, he knew how bad it was for the human body to function on periodic spells of sleep. But, he'd chosen this life, or perhaps it had chosen him. He wasn't built for a suit or tie, and he couldn't imagine spending hours of every day behind a desk or in a cubicle.

Plus, he got to save lives. Overall, he was okay with losing some sleep.

Shower first, he thought, heading for the doctors' lounge. Check his email, grab a sandwich, and then crash in the call room here at the hospital until he was called for the next emergency. Because there was always a next emergency.

He was powering up his phone when the click of heels distracted him. Nobody working in a hospital wore heels, except one person. *Tap, tap, tap.* Because he was looking down, those shoes came into his line of vision first. They were black and red, the heels do-me-baby high. They stopped moving and his gaze traveled as though it had a mind of its own to meet shapely ankles, lean, sexy calves, and a black skirt. She could be wearing a black, skintight, sexy top that showed a lot of cleavage. She could be wearing nothing at all on top. Impossible to tell, since she wore a crisp, white lab coat that was either brand new or recently ironed. When his gaze reached her face, he found her looking at him with the slightly irritated expression she always wore when she looked at him.

"Dr. Chance," he drawled. Even her makeup was perfect. Most of the women he worked with didn't have time or energy left over for foolish things like lipstick, but this one always looked fresh out of the salon. "You look like you just stepped off a fashion runway."

Her gaze traveled up and down his body, probably mimicking what he'd just done to hers, not that he meant to; he was simply too tired to control himself. "You look like you stepped out of a homeless shelter."

There were a lot of responses he could make to that.

6

He was trying to choose one from the tired jumble of his thoughts when his cell phone rang. Call display informed him that his best buddy was on the line. Normally he'd be only too happy to shoot the shit with Harvey but he had a bad feeling that his best friend wasn't calling to chat.

He contemplated ignoring the call but Rose Chance was regarding him with a level gaze that gave him the eerie sensation she could read his mind and knew all his secrets. Also, he was glad of an excuse not to have to talk to her—he didn't have the energy.

He clicked through to the call. "Hey man, what's up?"

"What's up yourself? You're hard to get a hold of."

"Oh, the usual." He might've laid it on a little thick about the number of emergency cases he'd been dealing with lately, and his overwhelming caseload, but knowing Rose was listing to every word stopped him.

"I'm checking that you've got the stag night under control."

He cursed inside his head. When he'd agreed to be best man at Harvey's wedding, he'd assumed that all he had to do was show up at the wedding, get the groom there on time, pass the ring, and make a speech. He'd had no idea that he would be called upon to organize a stag night.

"The stag. Yeah, absolutely. I'm on it." It wasn't that he'd forgotten the stag, he'd simply been swamped, and during the few snatched hours that weren't devoted to working or sleeping he'd had other, more important or more interesting things to do.

Rose didn't even pretend not to be listening. Those

big, deep blue eyes widened slightly. She tapped across to the fridge, opened it, and bent, treating him to a great view of the line of her hip. She withdrew a bottle of water and leaned against the counter openly watching him squirm.

"Good. Great," Harvey replied. "Not planning anything stupid, right? No strippers?"

Ah, so the call wasn't only to check up that Matt was doing his job but to ensure he was doing it properly. Harvey was a promising young lawyer with his sites clearly set on politics. Having grown up in the age of social media, they both knew that strippers were out of the question. "No peelers, I promise."

"Good. So? What are we doing?"

If only he wasn't so tired. His back hurt like hell, and the only few words he'd spoken in the last few hours were curt requests for the next instrument he needed. He hadn't powered up yet for social interaction. Or white lies. He rubbed his palm over his forehead as though he could massage the social part of his brain into action. "Well, obviously there's going to be drinking involved."

Rose shook her head, screwed the lid off her bottle of water and sipped as though it were a beer.

"Come on, dude. Tell me you've figured this out." A trace of irritation came across. Now that Harvey was confident the stag night wouldn't tarnish any future political career, he was all over the details.

"Of course I've got it figured out." His gaze bounced around the lounge, searching desperately for inspiration. He was too tired to make something up without help. Rose, regarding his discomfort, sipped more water. He saw a *Portland Now* magazine someone had left on a chair. The headline on the front cover advertised an article about the many microbreweries and craft breweries in the area. His tired brain latched on to the notion. Microbreweries. Yes! He said, "We're going on a pub-crawl. Check out a few microbreweries and craft breweries in the area."

Rose glanced at the magazine and back at him. He really wished she would find business elsewhere. It was bad enough performing under pressure without her scrutiny.

"Okay. That's cool. But a pub-crawl? That's it?" He knew his buddy liked to be different, but not too different. On the edge but never over it.

Desperation gave him a second idea. Possibly a stupid idea but he was too fatigued to judge. He made a gun with his thumb up and two fingers outstretched, closing one eye and pretending to squint down the barrel of a rifle. He aimed his imaginary firearm at Rose's heart. Her only reaction was to raise her eyebrows. "After we go shooting."

"Shooting?" There was silence for a second. Rose shook her head at him. And then Harvey laughed. "Shooting? Like a rifle range?"

"Handguns." He nodded, liking the idea. "We'll shoot for a couple hours, and then we hit the pub-crawl. Your stag will be unique."

"I gotta hand it to you, you came up with something perfect."

"Hey, my best friend only gets married once." Then he hesitated. "I hope."

Harvey laughed. "Oh, yeah. A woman like Theresa doesn't come along every day." He didn't have any more time to waste than Matt did. He said, "Thanks, bro. I'll see you for basketball Tuesday."

"You bet. Later."

He ended the call and Rose said, "How long have you been planning this stag night?"

She knew he'd come up with those ideas in the last couple of minutes and he knew she knew. He said, "Weeks."

Their gazes connected. There was something about this woman that always got under his skin. She wasn't even in the hospital that much, but he always seemed to be bumping into her with her perfect coolness, her unmussed beauty, and that sense she gave him that she thought he was beneath her.

He hailed from a Greek immigrant family. So what? Sure, his family never had any money and he'd worked as a waiter in a Greek restaurant to pay his way through school. She had blue blood pulsing through her veins. But no one knew better than a surgeon that when you get past the skin, blood's pretty much blood.

After gazing at him coolly for another moment, she said, "My brother is a cop. If you need to find a shooting gallery he can probably help."

He was so surprised he damn near dropped his new smartphone. First, because he'd imagined that if she had a brother he'd manage an investment firm on Wall Street or something rather than go into law enforcement. Second because she didn't seem like the kind of woman who would rush to help a guy in a jam. "Why would you help me?"

She tossed the now empty water bottle into the recycling container. "One day I'll need a favor. And you'll owe me."

Two

ROSE RETURNED TO the birthing room an hour later to check on her patient. The atmosphere was less positive than the last time she'd been in. Belinda looked exhausted, her damp hair was plastered to her forehead and Charlie had the beaten-down look of a man who's recently been yelled at.

"Okay," Rose said, stepping into the room, "looks like things are coming along." If she had to guess, she would say her patient was in transition, possibly the toughest part of labor when mentally the patient was struggling the most. To Rose, transition signaled that the final stage of labor was about to get underway.

"Let's take a look," she said, putting on a clean pair of surgical gloves and once more positioning the stool at the bottom of the birthing bed.

"This isn't like the other times," Belinda said. She was panting and Rose could hear distress in her tone. "It's taking longer and I feel like something's not working."

"Every birth is different," she said, speaking as

soothingly as she could.

But her examination revealed that, in fact, Belinda hadn't progressed very far, only another centimeter. "You're at eight centimeters. Not much farther to go." Belinda knew as well as she did that full dilation was ten centimeters. "Try walking around for a little bit," she suggested.

"We tried that," Belinda snarled at her. "I've trekked miles down this damn hospital corridor."

"Okay."

She glanced at Charlie. He said, "She's been getting a lot of contractions. Hard ones. Something's different."

Anita came in at that moment with a student nurse in tow. "I've run a hot tub for you. Sometimes that can help." At least it would give Belinda something to do, and the warm water should help relax her. "This is Tess, she's going to help you into the tub. I'll check on you in a few."

Rose didn't like the way this birth was more complicated than the previous three. She always listened to the mothers because they were the ones in touch with their own bodies. She was concerned that Belinda felt something was wrong. While Tess helped Belinda out of the bed and walked her slowly out of the room, Anita stayed behind to confer with Rose.

"What do you think?" Rose had learned a long time ago that astute nurses were among the best friends a doctor could have in the birthing room. There wasn't much they hadn't seen.

There was a crease of worry between her brows. "It's like her body's working so hard but the baby doesn't seem to be budging."

Rose nodded. "When she gets out of the tub, let's put her on a monitor and see what's going on with baby."

According to the monitor, the baby was doing okay; it was simply taking its time.

"I'm so tired," Belinda wailed.

"Our only other option would be a C-section."

She already knew that Belinda and Charlie had strong feelings about birthing naturally, but she wanted to float the idea.

"No," Belinda said. "Let's see if we can do this naturally."

"Sure."

They waited an hour, and then another hour, by which time Belinda was wearing down. "You're nearly fully dilated," Rose said, relieved things finally seemed to be happening. "Do you feel like pushing?"

"I feel like going home, opening a beer and pretending none of this ever happened," Belinda said.

"Well, if you're making jokes that's a good sign."

Belinda started pushing, and she kept pushing, she pushed until it was clear she was beyond exhaustion and only brute will was carrying her on. Rose never ceased to be amazed by the strength of women giving birth. Even though Charlie and Belinda had three children already, she was still amazed that such a very large man and such a tiny woman had mated. Love might be blind, but you'd think simple biology would rebel against her having children with such a big guy.

Tess, the student nurse, stayed with them. All of them, from Charlie to Anita to Rose to Tess, kept encouraging the laboring mother. At last Rose saw the head crowning. "I see the head," she said packing her words with encouragement. "We're almost there."

The nurses were ready to greet the newborn, everything was in place. With a huge cry of pain Belinda gave all she had as she pushed. The head emerged.

And there it stuck.

"Okay, another little push and we'll get the shoulders out."

Belinda grunted, pushing so hard her face grew deep red with effort. Nothing happened down below.

Rose and Anita exchanged a glance. It was clear to both of them that Belinda's strength was dwindling and all her pushing could not dislodge the baby's shoulders. In a low voice she said to the nurse, "We've got to do a crash section. Get me a neonatologist and let's get Belinda prepped for surgery."

Anita nodded and sped to the phone.

"What's happening?" Charlie asked.

Rose pulled in a deep breath so she would sound completely calm when she said, "Baby's shoulders are too wide. We're going to have to do a C-section after all."

"But the head's out!" Belinda cried.

She walked to the side of the bed and took Belinda's hand in both of hers. She gazed into the mother's eyes and saw the fear. Really hoped her own wasn't showing. "I need you to stay positive. We need to get your baby out, now. Okay?"

"How can you do a C-section when the baby's head is already out?" Belinda asked, her voice trembling.

"I'm sorry to tell you this, but the head is going back up the same way it came out. You're going to be sore tomorrow."

If she and the baby survived.

Rose had read about cases like this, but never been involved in one. And she could have lived her whole life without ever encountering this phenomenon.

"Charlie?" Belinda held out her hand and her husband gripped it in his huge paw.

"I'll be right here when you get out." Then he looked at Rose, so white with fear she thought he might faint. "You'll do it, right?"

"Yes, I'm caesarian certified."

He nodded.

In seconds, scrub nurses arrived to wheel Belinda to the OR while Rose prepped for surgery. She nearly knocked Matt to the floor when she ran in to scrub. "Hey, what's up?" he asked after one look at her face.

"Crash section. Baby's head came out and the shoulder's stuck."

He looked at her for a moment and she felt that he could see her tension. "Let me assist."

"Thanks." She had no time for more. They scrubbed up side-by-side and then walked together into the OR.

The anesthetist arrived and put Belinda under, and a surgical nurse intubated the unconscious woman.

"Have you done this before?" Matt asked. "With the head already out?"

"First time for everything." Their gazes connected and then she took a steadying breath, carefully grasped the baby's head and pushed it back up the birth canal. "Anita, I need you to hold the head in place. Let's go." She glanced at the big clock.

"We've got three minutes people," she snapped.

15

"Let's do this."

The prep nurse had put a film over the belly and there was a drape in place to catch fluids. Rose took a cautery scalpel and sliced through skin and fat, when she got to the abdominal rectus muscle, Matt and she pulled it apart. Then, while he retracted the bladder, she sliced oh, so carefully into the uterus, causing a big gush of fluid. Matt suctioned out fluid and blood to give her a clear view. He helped her expand the uterus and then she was able to grasp the head and get the baby out.

It was Matt who cut the umbilical cord, a job Charlie had been so looking forward to doing himself.

Rose sent up a silent prayer for that poor, big-shouldered baby and for the brave mother whose three kids needed her as she passed the babe to Anita who immediately took the baby to the neonatologist.

Matt pulled the layers of muscle and skin together while she sewed Belinda back up.

She felt they made a good team. Both were fast, careful, and efficient.

She was nearly done stitching when she heard a sound that brought tears to her eyes. The child began to cry.

"Good work, everyone," she said when she'd finished. Belinda's vitals were good and the baby was checking out fine.

"Nice work, doc," Matt said.

She glanced up at him over his mask, and with his mop of hair covered by his scrub cap, he was all eyes. Intense, brown eyes . "You too," she said.

She delivered the news to Charlie herself, that both his girls had come through the ordeal. He started to cry, big, slow tears that ripped at her. "You saved my wife, Rose. And our baby." He pulled her into an awkward hug. "God bless you."

"Anita will let you know when you can go in and see them both, but I wanted to let you know."

Rose did not leave the hospital until she was convinced that both her patients were doing well. Belinda, groggy from the anesthetic and the ordeal, looked exhausted but happy as her brand-new daughter suckled greedily at her breast. "What are you going to call her?" Rose asked.

Belinda smiled. "Now that I've seen those linebacker shoulders, I think we're to call her Dick Butkus."

"I guess she takes after her dad."

"I should've listened to my mother. She told me not to marry him. He's 6'5" and 250 and I'm 5'4" and 120, when I'm not pregnant."

"One thing's for sure. I bet you can talk him into that vasectomy now."

By the time Rose left the hospital she was running on adrenaline and the kind of spiky high that comes from getting through a life-and-death battle with life winning. As she hit the main lobby of the hospital, Matt was coming towards her wearing jeans, an old college sweatshirt, and sneakers with one lace dragging. His hair was wet where he'd clearly showered but he hadn't bothered to shave or comb his hair, so he looked as disreputable as always. But she didn't care.

He came towards her and she stopped to wait for him. There was a light in his eyes that she recognized because she suspected it was reflected in her own. They had beaten back death tonight and it felt good.

"Hey," he said.

"You did good work in there," she replied. "Thanks."

He shook his head. "I've read about that but, man, I had no idea I'd ever find myself helping push a baby back up the birth canal and doing an emergency C-section."

"Would you like to go for a drink?" When she heard the words she was surprised they had even come out of her mouth.

He appeared equally surprised. "You hitting on me, doc?"

Since he was obviously joking, she rolled her eyes. "As if. I tend to go for men who own a comb." She shook her head helplessly. "It's kind of a thank you for stepping up tonight. Also, I feel so keyed up and so restless I'm not ready to go home. I've been working fourteen hours straight but I feel like I could go on for another fourteen."

He nodded. "It's the adrenaline." He seemed to hesitate. A duffel bag hung from his right hand and she thought maybe he had someone waiting for him. She knew nothing about his personal life. Not that she'd ever had an interest in it. Feeling suddenly foolish she said, "Forget I asked. It was a crazy idea."

"No. I'm down. We should go."

"Okay then."

"In fact, there's a fantastic craft brewery only a couple of blocks from here. Nothing like a long, cold glass of local brew after a hard day at the office."

"I'm guessing you only discovered the existence of this brewery when you grabbed up that issue of *Portland Now*. Plus, you can check out the venue for the bachelor party you are supposed to be organizing."

He looked crestfallen, but a disturbing glint lurked in the depths of his eyes. "Am I that transparent?"

"Like a plate glass window."

Three

THE BREWERY WAS called Hazel Nut's, and as they walked in the air was warm and humid from damp rain jackets and, presumably, beer brewing. They settled at a table so roughhewn her dad could have built it.

The available beers were listed on a chalkboard along with a menu of local breads, cheeses, and charcuterie. Their main brew seemed to be, not surprisingly, a hazelnut-flavored beer.

"What do you think?" Matt asked, also perusing the menu. "You could get a flight of beers and try out three. They all seem to be honey, nut, or chocolate flavored."

"I'll go with a pint of hazelnut. I'm not sure I could stomach a flight of nut beers."

"Sounds good." And without another word he headed for the bar and ordered them a couple of pints. There was a waitress taking a large order at a big corner table, but Matt was obviously not a person who liked to wait around for something he could get himself.

When he returned with two tall, cold glasses of hazelnut brew, she felt a moment of awkwardness. The only thing they had in common was work, and now that they were away from the hospital she didn't want to talk about the hospital. Intuitively, she knew that Matt didn't either.

He took a sip of his beer, contemplated it the way a sommelier would taste a 1948 Château Lafite Rothschild, and then nodded.

"Does it meet with your approval?"

"Yeah. It's pretty good. You?"

"It tastes like beer." She settled back in her chair and eased her feet inside the killer pumps. "Well? Will this place do as one of the stops in your beer crawl?"

"Yeah." He glanced around. "Plenty of places to sit, good vibe, good beer. What more do you want?"

She didn't hesitate. "Drivers. You want a team of designated drivers."

He seemed impressed at her suggestion. "Good point. Hadn't really thought that through."

"How many guys will be attending this stag?"

He shrugged. Something else she suspected he hadn't thought through. She watched him do the mental math. "Twenty, give or take. My buddy Harvey has a lot of friends locally."

Her eyes widened slightly at mention of the groom's name. "Maybe you should rent a minibus with a driver."

A gleam of respect shone in his eyes. "That's a fantastic idea." He pulled out his smart phone and made a note, then glanced up at her. "I don't suppose you know any minibuses and drivers do you?"

She couldn't help the amusement that bubbled up, as it had been doing since he mentioned the first name of the groom. "As a matter fact, I do. I recently hired one for the hen party I'm organizing." She leaned back and sipped her beer. It was supposed to taste like the hazelnuts that grew so abundantly in Oregon.

Matt might dress like a schlep, but his brain was as sharp as the creases in an Armani suit. His eyes were the color of good dark chocolate. "You're organizing a hen party?"

"Quite a coincidence."

He tipped back in his chair, looking amused. "It's the same wedding, isn't it?"

"Is your buddy Harvey marrying a woman named Theresa?" When he nodded, she put up her hands, fingers spread open.

"Small world. How do you know Theresa?"

"We're from the same town. Hidden Falls, Oregon. We were friends through school, went our separate ways for college and then bumped into each other one day in Powell's. Turned out we were reading the same book for our book clubs." She smiled at the memory. "Theresa had barely changed at all. And, when you've known someone your whole life, it's like you can not see each other for years and then you bump into each other and pick right up again.

"It's strange we haven't run into each other socially with them."

"I know. But when two people become a couple they usually socialize with other couples." Even as she said the words, she realized that they made her sound like a sad, lonely woman with no social life.

The truth was she wasn't sad or lonely, but she had just let Matt know she was single. Crap. She'd run through a deep mud puddle in her new shoes before

22

she'd let him think she was interested in him.

With a display of tact she wouldn't have thought he stocked, he didn't comment.

Of course, if he was socializing with Harvey and Theresa, then he was likely in a relationship.

Whatever.

"How about you?" she asked him. "How did you and Harvey meet?"

"The woman I was seeing at the time was best friends with the woman Harvey was seeing at the time. Neither of those relationships lasted, but Harvey and I did." He grinned. "I moved to Portland for the job and Harvey was the guy who invited me into his pick-up basketball league. We hung out a lot when we were both single. We were out together the night he met Theresa." He snapped his fingers and pulled out his phone once again. "Also at a bar. I'll add that to the list."

"The Hedgeman?"

"On your list, too?"

"Great minds."

He leaned in and put his hands on the table. Sent her a Gary Cooper at High Noon glance. "My shooting range is going to be way cooler than yours."

She laughed. Genuinely amused. "I can't imagine going to a shooting gallery with Theresa. I'd be in fear for my life."

Theresa was a fun and spontaneous woman, but she was also the kind of person who forgot what she was doing when she had a thought she wanted to share. Rose pictured her with the trigger half depressed suddenly turning to Rose to tell her something important she'd just thought of.

Matt obviously knew Theresa well enough to get the joke. "I definitely don't want you to go to a hen party and end up on my operating table."

Their gazes connected and she felt a strange jolt of awareness. Not that there was anything sexy about an operating table, but, well, sizzle was sizzle. And strangely, the two of them had it tonight. Most likely this absurd attraction was the result of the emotional highs of delivering a healthy baby and getting Belinda Tate through the ordeal safely.

Not that she had any interest in Matt women-fall-at-my-feet Vasilopolous, tonight or any night. She took a sip of beer.

He did the same. "Is your brother really a cop?"

"Yes, he really is."

"I figured you were from a family of bluebloods. I guess, if I thought about it all, I'd have imagined your brother would run his own hedge fund or something."

She was amused, but not surprised. Rose had consciously set herself apart from her family when she was young and everything about them embarrassed her. Now she'd been doing it unconsciously for so many years that she supposed she projected the background she wished she'd had rather than the one she grew up in. She never lied about her past, though.

"My family is about as far from high-class as, say, Paris, France is from Paris, Texas. My parents are truly amazing people. Loving, giving, the kind of folks public television makes documentaries about." And at least that was one horror she had been spared.

"Seriously?"

She nodded. "My 19-year-old mom was already

pregnant when she met my dad." She smiled. "Jack is the kind of man who is all heart and no practical sense. They got married, had the kid and then sort of collected more children."

She could feel his attention on her. His focus grew more intense. "Collected children?"

"Yes. In rural Oregon in the 70s and 80s there were communes and loads of alternative people going around in bare feet wearing hemp clothes and living off the land with no skills. Naturally, they started having children." Mostly she had contempt for these people; contempt for anyone who brought children into the world without being ready. She'd long ago realized that her parents were much nicer than she was. "Word got around that if you had a kid you didn't know what to do with, maybe didn't want anymore, Jack and Daphne were your people. It was like a no-kill dog shelter for kids. And meanwhile, they were having their own babies, so we ended up with a family of eleven kids."

"Wow. You sound pretty hostile."

"More frustrated. Of course, I think they're wonderful people and what they did was amazing and generous. But growing up as one of eleven children wasn't easy. We always had plenty to eat and lots of love but I hated feeling poor." She made a face. "Wearing hand-me-down clothes that were awful to start with."

He was nodding as though he knew what she was talking about. "Not enough attention, right? Not enough money for field trips, or the new sneakers everybody had, but the discount store brand was good enough for you."

It was her turn to be surprised. "Wow, you've been

there."

He grinned. "And have the emotional scars to prove it." He pushed back his chair, also pushing back from the statement he'd just made. "Not really. My folks emigrated from Greece with nothing. Barely any English, next to no money, all they had on their side was youth and a naïve belief that everyone in America could be rich. Luckily they were also willing to work hard."

The easy response was to say that it must've worked out pretty well for them since their son was a surgeon. But one thing Rose's background had taught her was that the easy response was so often the wrong one. She asked, "How many in your family?"

He laughed. "Compared to your folks, mine were rank amateurs. Only five kids. But when you grow up hearing how your parents struggled to give their children all the advantages of growing up American, how they sacrificed so you could have the opportunities and education they were denied—and don't forget that old chestnut that everybody in America can be rich—well, you end up pretty driven to succeed."

"Are all the kids in your family successful?"

"Yeah, pretty much. One brother's a lawyer, one sister's an engineer, my other sister designs websites. My younger brother worked in a Greek restaurant. Well, we all did. We speak Greek and we know how to work hard. I put myself through school thanks to the Greek place and student loans, but my youngest brother, Alexei, he started his own food truck."

She put her beer down so it made a thunk. "Alexei's? In that whole block of food trucks? Is that your brother's?"

He nodded, looking proud that she knew of his brother's place.

"That place is amazing. I grab his lamb souvlaki combo all the time."

"I know. He's got four trucks and plans to expand."

"I'll have to tell him I know you next time I go there. Maybe he'll give me a discount."

Matt laughed. "He'll more likely charge you double."

"Sibling rivalry?"

"You have no idea."

Amazingly, from believing they'd have nothing to talk about she found they had a lot in common, even to being attendants in the same wedding. "You're really going shooting? For your stag party?"

He shrugged. "You saw me grasping at straws. I only got the idea from the cover of that magazine, but Harvey seemed to like the idea of shooting guns to celebrate a wedding. What do you think?"

"Actually, I think it's really cool of you and I'm serious, if you have trouble finding a place, my brother knows them all."

"Thanks. How about you? What are the girls going to be doing for their stagette?"

"I'm not telling."

He flashed a grin that probably made women drop their panties in droves. "Come on. I won't tell. Male strippers?"

She rolled her eyes. "Oh please. Remember, I'm organizing this."

"Right. Dr. Vogue is organizing a hen party." He narrowed his gaze then looked at her as though he could see right into her thoughts. Even though she knew he couldn't, the close scrutiny made her wish she'd taken five extra minutes to freshen her makeup before meeting him here. "You're going to a fashion show."

She laughed and shook her head. But to give the guy credit, he wasn't too far off. She'd arranged with her favorite high-end lingerie boutique for a private, after-hours showing of the latest in high-end sexy sweet nothings. All the women had chipped in so the bride would have a certain amount of money to spend on lingerie. Rose was fairly certain the rest of the women would do some shopping while they were there, too.

"Come on," he wheedled, "I told you what I'm doing."

She shook her head. "No, I happened to be present when desperation made you grab the first idea you saw."

"Luckily, I perform well under pressure."

Four

THERESA STANFORD WAS one of the bubbliest people Rose had ever known. But there was champagne bubbly and there was a kid taking a straw and blowing bubbles into a glass of milk bubbly. Most of the time, Theresa was the good kind of bubbly. But sometimes, Rose felt little splatters of milk landing on her arms. "So, I hear you and Matt Vasilopolous know each other," she said in a loud voice right in the middle of *Bride Knows Best*.

The women of the bridal party were bridesmaid dress shopping. Rose was too busy to shop, and Theresa had assured her that they could choose something without her, but Rose had carved out time by skipping her Saturday workout. Better a hint of cellulite than being stuck with a butt-ugly dress. "Yes. We do."

"It is such a small world." They were currently flipping through catalogues and looking at samples at the boutique where Theresa had chosen her wedding gown.

"Yeah. I have admitting privileges to the same hospital where he works. We don't know each other well, we're colleagues."

Theresa nudged her with an elbow. "He says you're an interesting woman." She said it in a sly tone, as though Rose ought to be thrilled.

Rose's hand tightened on the satin sleeve of the green gown she was assessing. She liked the straight, simple cut, but when she tried to picture all of the bridesmaids together she suspected they'd look like spears of asparagus. She turned her head. "Interesting woman? That's what he said about me?"

No doubt hearing the disdain in her tone, Theresa said, "Interesting is good."

Not that she cared what Matt thought of her, but 'an interesting woman' was the sort of thing you'd say about a politician you admired, a feminist activist, or an author whose books you didn't really understand who was being interviewed on television. Rose tried not to let vanity rule her life, but she was accustomed to hearing herself described in terms like beautiful, fascinating, or, at the very least, attractive. But interesting?

She felt like a maiden aunt who'd enjoyed a long career as an archaeologist.

"And what did you think of him?" Theresa asked in that same coy tone, like a matchmaker about to score. Rose had no idea why it happened, but it seemed like the second one of her friends became engaged she turned into a determined matchmaker. Maybe it was because she wanted all her friends to be just as happy as she was, or perhaps she simply wanted her single friends to become her married friends. Either way, the engaged woman trying to marry off her friends was a phenomenon Rose found particularly distasteful.

Especially now, and with Matt.

"I think he needs to get on better terms with his hairbrush and his razor," she said, hoping to nip any matchmaking ideas in the bud.

The nipping did not work. "I know!" Theresa gushed. "He's got that sexy, sleepy look, like he's too busy saving lives to bother with personal grooming."

"You've been watching too much *Grey's Anatomy*. Trust me, even a busy surgeon has time to shave."

Not that she had any interest in him herself, but Rose was curious about whether Matt had a girlfriend or not. She wished she knew how to ask without Theresa thinking she was interested. Luckily, Sarah, one of the other bridesmaids, piped up from behind a row of bridal veils so she looked like a ghostly silhouette. "I heard he's really hot. Is he single?"

Every one of the bridesmaids' heads turned to hear Theresa's response. The bride-to-be shrugged. "I think his social media profile would read, 'it's complicated.' I'm pretty sure there is a woman in his life, but I get the feeling it's casual." Rose knew all about casual relationships. It was so tough to keep a relationship going and build a career in medicine.

Sarah pondered the words, as, Rose suspected, the rest of them were. All of Theresa's bridesmaids were single. "So, he's available?" Sarah asked.

"I say, knock yourself out."

Rose spent the next thirty minutes using all her tact, as well as her years of staying on top of fashion trends and her natural sense of style to guide Theresa and the other women towards bridesmaid gowns that didn't make them look like some version of tropical fruit.

Since it was a February wedding, which, even in the rainy Pacific Northwest, was considered winter, the fashion was for bold colors. Reds, blues, and greens. Luckily, none of the bridesmaids was interested in frills and bows and poofs. Eventually, they all settled on navy blue dresses that were figure hugging without being too sexy.

There were samples of the dress hanging in the boutique, and one was in Rose's size. She stripped off her cherry-red sweater, designer jeans and her favorite black boots and slipped into the sample.

As she contemplated her reflection in the change room mirror, and watched the way it hugged her curves, she decided that no one looking at her in this dress would think of her as an interesting woman.

They ordered the dresses. The most important decision made, the five women headed out shoe shopping. What they wanted was a shoe they could all fall in love with, and all wear again. The perfect pair was surprisingly easy to find. They were from one of the less expensive designers; low heeled enough that no one would be toppling, but stylish, too, with a small blue satin bow—fortunately removable—perched over the toes.

During lunch she got to know the other bridesmaids better. Sarah was a talkative, nosy, noisy woman who worked for a bank. Kimberly was her opposite in every way. A quiet, shy woman who Rose had never met before. She said little, not that anyone could get a word in with Sarah and Theresa around. She had pale blonde hair and soft features, and seemed to shrink into herself if asked a question. She was a cousin of Theresa's and

Rose got the feeling that she'd been forced into being a bridesmaid by her family. The final bridesmaid was Marta, a cheerful Mexican who laughed at all of Theresa's jokes. Rose could see why they were friends. All of them laughed as they related various horror stories from weddings they'd attended.

When she was half way through her Cobb salad, her younger brother James texted her wanting to meet up.

In Portland on cop business, he texted.

Coffee?

Of course she didn't have time for coffee, but then she didn't see James nearly as often as she'd like. She texted back.

Sure. Come pick me up.

She gave him the name and address of the restaurant. Theresa was telling them a story of how she'd almost lost her engagement ring down the kitchen sink and Stephen King himself couldn't have imbued the tale with more horror or suspense, when James walked in the door of the restaurant.

He was in his uniform. Even though he was her brother she took a second to admire how handsome he looked. There was something about a good-looking man in uniform. As he strode toward them, Kimberly made a tiny sound. Rose assumed she was also noticing that a hottie in uniform was approaching, but when she glanced at her fellow bridesmaid she saw her eyes were wide and her cheeks even more pale than usual. She seemed to shrink back in her seat and for a second Rose was worried she might faint.

She introduced James to the women he didn't already know.

"Good afternoon, ladies," he said in his cheerful way.

"Why Sherriff Chance," Sarah said, tossing her hair back over her shoulder. "Are you here to arrest us for having a good time?"

He laughed as though it were the first time anyone had made a joke like that. "No, ma'am." He leaned closer and she saw Sarah go into full flirting mode. "But don't jaywalk or I will have to get out the cuffs."

He turned to say hi to the rest of the women and Sarah leaned into Theresa and said in a voice that was probably meant to be quiet, "When he said 'cuffs' I had a total *Fifty Shades of Grey* moment."

James, naturally, pretended he hadn't heard. He shook hands with everyone and got to Kimberly last. When he held out his hand hers trembled visibly. She barely even murmured a greeting. James looked at her for a moment, his cheerful grin fading. He glanced at Rose, who shrugged. She had no idea what was going on with Kimberly.

She'd have asked him to join them but Kimberly looked as though she were about to slide beneath the table. They'd taken in a stray dog once when they were kids and poor Lady was terrified of the mail carrier and anyone in uniform. She was getting the same vibe from Kimberly. She'd finished her meal anyway, so she stood and said, "I have to go. This has been great. Can't wait to see you all at the hen party."

She walked out with James and he said, "What was up with the pretty blonde, Kimberly?"

"I don't know. She reminded me of Lady. Remember that dog?"

He nodded. "The one who was scared of anyone wearing a uniform." He strode forward with his purposeful gait. "But is that a thing? In humans?"

"I don't know. Mostly I deal with ear infections and pregnant ladies."

"I don't usually scare beautiful women."

Beautiful? She wouldn't have called Kimberly beautiful, but then James always went for wounded doves and underdogs. She leaned into him. "On the plus side, you did give Sarah a *Fifty Shades* moment."

"Don't even go there."

"So what's this cop business that brings you into Portland on a Saturday?"

"There's a thing. A joint task force. Not even sure I'll be appointed to it, this was an introductory meeting."

He was deliberately vague which, she knew, meant he wasn't going to tell her more. Interesting.

"Where do you want to go for coffee?" he asked.

"I don't have a lot of time. I need to run into the hospital and check on a couple of patients."

"Then how about here?" He indicated an indie coffee place with a big sign that boasted the best cinnamon buns in Portland.

"Perfect."

They entered and she experienced the slight ruffle in the atmosphere that always happened when she was with her brother and he was in uniform. She felt the breathless moment when everyone reviewed their personal criminal record. Did they have unpaid parking tickets? Would he be able to tell? When they were settled at a small table near the back, she had a good look at her brother.

He was funny and charming, but he also had a serious side. When he'd gone into policing she'd been both surprised and worried. Surprised that anyone who grew up in the extremely liberal Chance household would go into a profession that was completely dominated by structure and hierarchy and was, in fact, part of 'the system' that their father, Jack Chance, was always railing against.

When James moved to Seattle to work for their PD she'd imagined he'd work his way up in the ranks and end up as the chief one day. Instead, when the old sheriff of Hidden Falls had announced his retirement, James had decided to run for the office.

He was the ideal candidate. Young, smart, well-trained, and, more important in a small town, likable. He preferred compromise to confrontation and seemed content to keep peace in the much smaller, quieter world of Hidden Falls.

He'd never talked much about his work in Seattle but she knew he'd dealt with some grisly cases and was somewhat impatient with all the bureaucracy. Hidden Falls had never had a crime more grisly than schoolyard fistfights and messy road accidents. And, unlike his Seattle work, James loved to talk about his current cases. "So," she said, "What's the latest in the dark criminal underbelly of Hidden Falls?"

James placed his elbows on the table and leaned forward, dropping his voice so no one in the vicinity could overhear them. "Had a pretty ugly confrontation between Winnifred and Joel Parsons and Reggie Banger."

She knew the Parsons, they'd been in Hidden Falls

forever. An annoying pair of killjoys she'd always thought. They were the kind of people who turned their lights out and pretended they weren't home when Christmas carolers came calling. "I don't think I know Reggie Banger."

"He's a newcomer. Only been in Hidden Falls about five years."

"That's why I haven't met him. I've been gone at least that long."

"He's not the Parsons' kind of people. Works from home, so they are convinced he's a drug dealer, which they've informed me of many times."

"Is he?" She knew there were some old potheads in the area, who grew marijuana in their back yards for their own use, but a drug dealer?

"No. He telecommutes. He's a programmer."

"What was the confrontation about? His alleged drug dealing?"

"His vicious dog."

"You can't blame the dog, you have to look at the owner," she said, parroting one of their mother's sayings.

"Yeah. And they did look at the owner. Harsh words were exchanged, some ugly insults, and they threatened to sue him."

"They wanted to sue their neighbor for a barking dog?"

"Yep." He was starting to grin, and she couldn't help but join in even though she didn't yet know why this was a grinning matter. "He called me and wanted to press charges. Trespassing and harassment."

His eyes were twinkling. "I went over to try and

37

talk some sense into both of them. And you know what?"

"I'm on the edge of my seat."

"There is no dog."

"What? Did he get rid of it?"

"No. He never had one. He's working on a home safety device. Dog barking sounds that get triggered if he's not home and anyone approaches the house."

"Kind of like a motion detector light?"

"Exactly like that. And the longer the intruder hangs around, the fiercer the dog barks."

She was beginning to realize how much she missed Hidden Falls. "And the Parsons were snooping around his yard when he wasn't home, triggering the frenzied barks."

"Yep."

"Sometimes, I really miss that place."

"You could always move back. You know we need a local doc."

"Not that much."

He sipped coffee. "So? What's up with you?"

She told him about Belinda's terrifying birth ordeal and he was duly impressed. "That is the single grossest thing I've ever heard."

"It was terrifying at the time." She thought for a second. "I never realized how similar our work is. Both involve a lot of boring, routine days punctuated with spells of action and terror."

"Yep, pretty much." He sipped some coffee then said, "So, you dating anyone?"

"Nope. You?"

He shook his head. "I got my heart broken when I

fell for Holly Legere and she chose my decamillionaire architect brother over me. I may never recover."

Her lips twitched. "I was there, remember? You were flirting with her like crazy under Scott's nose, being a shit disturber."

He chuckled. "Haven't had that much fun since we were kids. Man we used to pull some pranks on each other, didn't we?"

She shuddered. "So, your heart wasn't exactly broken."

"No, but she was the coolest girl I've seen in a while. If she wasn't all over Scott I probably would have asked her out. Maybe."

She ran a fingertip around the thick rim of her pottery mug. "Can I ask you something?"

"Sure."

"If you referred to a woman as *interesting*, what would that mean?"

A look of disgust crossed his face. "I would never call a woman interesting. A woman is hot or not hot. Then single or not single, and so on."

"So, you'd never call a hot, single woman *interesting*."

"Well, if she was a scientist or something and explained quantum physics in a way I could understand it. That would be interesting."

"Hah. I knew it," she exclaimed as though she'd won an argument.

James loved a joke and she felt that he was enjoying one at her expense at this very moment. "So, my detective skills are kind of rusty, but did a hot guy call you *interesting* recently?"

"Yes. One did."

He shook his head. "Ouch."

Five

WHEN THE COFFEE was drunk and she and James had caught up on each other's latest, she said, "I hate to run, but I have to go and check on a patient."

"Yeah. I should be getting back, too."

They said their goodbyes and she headed to the hospital. Belinda wasn't bouncing back after the long labor and the cesarean and Rose wanted to check on her, as well as two other patients who were in hospital. One after gall bladder surgery and one about tests for possible cancer.

When she got to Belinda's room she paused on the threshold, her eyebrows raised in surprise. Matt was sitting beside Belinda, chatting to her as though they were old friends, the newest Tate baby asleep in his arms. He wore surgical scrubs, needed a shave, and a comb dragged through the dark curls on his head, but she still felt the inevitable *oh that's so adorable* feeling of seeing a full-grown, virile man holding a sleeping newborn.

"Hi," she said as she walked in.

"Hi Rose," Belinda said.

Matt merely nodded.

She picked up Belinda's chart and scanned it. "How are you feeling?"

"Tired," Belinda admitted. Then she looked over at Matt and grinned. "Look, Pippin's got her first boyfriend."

"Pippin? Is that baby's name?"

Belinda nodded. "I was eating a Cox's Red Pippin apple when I went into labor. We grow them on our property. It was Charlie's idea to call her Pippin. She damned near killed me, but at least she's an easy baby."

"Rose, good to see you," Matt said. "You usually work weekends?"

Right, because she was so *interesting* she had nothing better to do on a Saturday than hang around the hospital. "I was out shopping for bridal wear with Theresa and the rest of the bridesmaids, and then we went for lunch. I'm only stopping in quickly to check on Belinda and a couple of other patients before heading out for the evening."

"Sounds like fun."

Or like she was trying to make herself come across as social and busy. What was she doing? What did she care what he thought? If he believed she was an interesting woman why should she try and change his mind? It wasn't like she was *interested* in him.

Belinda might be tired, but she was obviously getting stronger every day. "Can I go home, Rose? I miss my kids."

Pippin was doing great. She wasn't only big in the shoulders, she was big everywhere, and didn't seem to have suffered any ill effects from her calamitous beginning. "Do you have help at home?"

"My mother's looking after the kids while I'm in here. She'll come and help out. Plus, Charlie's really good."

She nodded, relieved to find Belinda wasn't going to be wearing herself out when she was still so weak. "If you promise me to rest every day. Have a nap when Pippin sleeps, and let your mother and Charlie take over the cooking and cleaning. Then yes, I think you could go home tomorrow."

The baby stirred at that moment and started to fuss. Matt stood, gracefully, as though screaming babies were no big deal. He passed the baby to its mother. She prepared to nurse and, after wishing her well, he headed for the door. Rose followed him out.

She turned to him when they were out in the hall with no chance that Belinda could overhear them. "Well, what do you think?"

"I think it's a good thing she wasn't eating a Golden Delicious when she went into labor."

She snorted with laughter. "I mean, what do you think about her health? When I saw you there, I thought maybe you were worried about her. Am I letting her go home too early?"

"No. I like to check on a patient sometimes, that's all." He shrugged, looking uncomfortable. "I know we're not supposed to let this get personal. But saving lives is personal."

She nodded, surprised to find he felt that way.

They trod down the corridor, both sidestepping an orderly mopping the floor with practiced efficiency.

They diverged around the swooshing mop, she to the left and he to the right, and then met back again in the middle and continued on their way. "So," he said. "Your brother."

"My brother?"

"Yeah. The firearms range I want to get into said you have to be a member. When I called they said a lot of law enforcement personnel practice there. I was wondering whether your brother might be able to help us."

"Sure. I was with him an hour ago. I could have asked him then." She pulled out her cell phone and ducked into an empty lounge containing four easy chairs and a TV that was off. "What's the name of the facility?"

"Fennimen's Shooting Range."

She found James's number in her contact list and made the call. He answered right away, "Hey, Doc, how's my favorite sister?"

She smiled at his cheerful tone. "I bet you say that to all your sisters."

"Oh no. You are my favorite sister because you're the only one who never asks for favors." Since James was a genuine handyman, as opposed to their poor father whose favorite tool was the sledgehammer, and who had a bad habit of destroying things before he figured out how to rebuild them, James ended up getting a lot of please-can-you-help-me-fix-Dad's-mistake calls.

Since he was also the newly installed Sheriff of Hidden Falls, he'd also become the go-to guy for everything from flooding in the road outside their folks' place to their sister Marguerite being recently convinced she had a prowler. James had driven over in the middle of the night to confront the terrifying creature—a raccoon that had taken control of Marguerite's garage and wasn't giving it up without a fight.

She sighed. "And there goes my favorite sister status."

"No. Don't tell me. Imaginary stalkers, barking dogs, crazed animals taking over your garage. Those are not my jurisdiction. I can give you the number for the Portland PD."

"Actually, I do want a phone number. No, more than that. Do you have any pull with Fennimen's Shooting Club?"

"You taking up shooting now? Damn, you are definitely still my favorite sister."

"It's not for me." Briefly, she explained the situation and James said, "This guy you're helping out, this Matt, is he someone you can vouch for?"

She glanced across the small lounge at Matt who stood there, scruffy as always, watching her. "Well, he's a surgeon, so he is good with his hands, but I can't promise he won't shoot himself in the foot."

James laughed. "He better not shoot anybody in the foot or I'll have to arrest him."

"So you'll help?"

"Sure. I'll be heading back down there anyway one day this week. Tell your friend to get in touch and we'll figure something out."

"Thanks. Hey, you know who my favorite brother is?"

He chuckled. "I am not falling into that trap. We both know your favorite is Josh, because he's the only one in the family who cares about fashion the way you do."

It was her turn to laugh. "See you, second favorite brother."

She clicked her phone off. Glanced up at Matt. "Get your phone out. I'll give you James's number. He's willing to meet you down there and help you get a booking."

"Just text me his number."

She rolled her eyes. "You don't have my number."

"I know. If you text me his number then I'll have both of them."

She narrowed her gaze at him. "Why would you want my phone number?"

She was fairly certain she saw three possible responses to her question cross his face before he finally answered. "Because I may need to ask you some questions about this wedding."

She sighed. "Your mom and sisters do all your dirty work, don't they?"

He looked at her suspiciously. "Why do you say that?"

"Because I am going to do all the work of organizing your stag. And you'll get all the credit. Typical little-brother behavior."

She shook her head as she punched his number into her phone and then texted him James's contact info. "Boys," she muttered.

Six

BOYS? MATT'S GAZE followed as Dr. Vogue made her way out of the room, her heeled boots clacking a tattoo of disapproval. Boys? Was that really how she saw him? As a hopeless kid always in need of an older sis to help him out of a jam?

Not that he was above getting help, but he did not want Rose Chance seeing him as a boy. He definitely saw her as a woman and would really like it if, when she turned her stunning, sapphire eyes his way she saw a man standing in front of her.

He stomped out behind her, and might have brooded over how to change her mind except that his pager went off. Blood and mayhem called. Taking off at a jog, he had to go on manly business to save lives. He didn't have time to worry about what one sexy GP thought of him.

The emergency turned out to be a massive heart attack victim who needed an emergency coronary bypass. When he got into the chest cavity he discovered four blockages. After he'd finished, he took a long, hot shower. In the doctors' lounge he turned on his cell and called James Chance, and was asked to leave a message, which he did.

Then he headed to the cafeteria and settled at a table with an ER surgeon, Vin Shah, and an anesthetist, Bill Topley.

"So, you in for Friday night?" Bill asked him.

He could barely remember what day it was, never mind what he was supposed to do Friday. "Friday night?"

"Yeah. Poker with the boys."

Boys again. The word rankled. "I'll get back to you on that."

* * *

MONDAY WAS ALWAYS a busy day for Rose as all her patients who'd come down with something on the weekend or injured themselves wanted to see her. Rose tried to limit seeing patients to her posted office hours, but it wasn't easy. Today was a perfect example. A mom came in for her annual check up and dragged in two of her kids, one with an ear infection and one who had a severe case of tonsillitis. So, she didn't see one patient. She saw three. She never understood why people thought a busy doctor could squeeze in a couple of extra kids. Did they think because they were small they took up less of her time?

Lunch had been a salad from the deli downstairs, grabbed at three o'clock, then she'd dealt with not only her regular patients but a couple of walk-ins. A bladder infection and the victim of a fairly minor car accident.

Finally, at nearly five-thirty, as she was tidying up her desk, her receptionist/nurse rang through. "I've got one more patient for you, Dr. Chance."

Since Deirdre did not add patients after the office was officially closed, she knew this was no ordinary patient. "Who is it, Deirdre?"

"It's your father."

Her eyes opened wide. Her father wasn't one of her patients. She suspected he wanted to surprise her and take her out for sushi or something, so she smiled and said, "Send him in."

But when Jack Chance entered her office it was clear he didn't have sushi on his mind. "Dad? What's the matter? You look awful." His skin was gray and he seemed completely out of it.

"I don't know. I don't feel good. I'm dizzy. Didn't want to worry your mother."

He barely got to the word mother when he passed out. She ran forward, grabbing him before he hit the floor, yelling for Deirdre.

She did an EKG immediately, and as she'd feared she saw an abnormal heart rhythm. "I suspect a third degree heart block," she said to Deirdre as she called 911.

Her dad came to while she was doing his EKG. He looked surprised to see her.

"Did you drive all this way? By yourself?"

The man was barely functioning, how he'd driven more than sixty miles was beyond comprehension.

"I wasn't feeling this bad when I started out," he said. "I was planning to invite you out for dinner." He panted out the words. "Surprise you."

She smiled at him. "You sure did surprise me. Ambulance is on its way. Let's get you to hospital."

He hated hospitals but was too ill to argue. After the paramedics hooked him up with oxygen and strapped him into a stretcher, she jumped into her car and raced the few minutes to the hospital.

When she got to the ER, it was blessedly quiet. She consulted with Vin Shah, the emergency doc who ordered a full rainbow of blood tests and another EKG. He said, "He's got cardiomyopathy. Your dad just bought himself a pacemaker."

She nodded. "Who's the cardio-thoracic surgeon on duty?"

"Dr. Ogilvie."

Dr. Ogilvie was near retirement age and his best years were long behind him in Rose's opinion. No way he was cutting into the man she loved most in all the world. She exchanged a glance with Vin. "Where's Matt Vasilopolous?"

"He was here earlier. Think he's gone off shift."

She grabbed Vin's arm and lowered her voice. "Dr. Ogilvie is not operating on my father. Do not think about calling him. Give me ten minutes."

She hauled out her cell and rang Matt. Straight to voice mail which meant his phone was probably off.

She ran out and checked his schedule. He'd gone off shift ten minutes ago.

She sprinted, faster than she'd ever run in her life, to the call room. She was positive he wouldn't leave without showering off the grunge of the day. As little as she knew him, she knew this was his routine.

"Matt!" she yelled when she got there.

She heard singing above the sounds of a shower running. The singing was not in English. "Matt!" she yelled again.

The water turned off. "What?"

Oh, thank God. "I need you."

"Rose?"

"Yes. Hurry!" Fear and anxiety churned within her.

He didn't answer. But in less than twenty seconds stepped out of the shower with a towel wrapped around his waist and water still running down his skin where he hadn't taken the time to dry himself.

"What is it?"

"It's my dad. He needs emergency surgery." She gulped air and forced herself to calm down. "He needs a pacemaker. Please, can you do it?"

He blinked water out of his eyes. "I've just finished twelve hours. I'm not sure I–"

"Please, Matt. The cardio-thoracic surgeon on duty is Ogilvie. I can't let him cut my dad. I need you."

Their gazes connected. Wordlessly, he nodded. "Get me clean scrubs."

He stepped back into the cubicle and while he dried off, she grabbed a clean set of scrubs from the supply cupboard and passed them to him.

When she sprinted back to Emergency, Matt was at her side.

Rose did not like feeling helpless, but she was helpless. After racing back to emergency, filling Matt in along the way with her father's condition, she was able to introduce Jack Chance to his surgeon. Matt pushed the wheeled bed himself and she walked beside him right up to the doors to the surgical unit. Here Matt stopped. "This is as far as you go, Doc," he told her.

She nodded and moved closer to her dad. She leaned in and grabbed his shoulder, held on. "I'll be right here when you wake up," she told him.

He answered with a weak smile. "Don't worry your mother. She'll only fuss."

She turned to the man who'd gone back to work after twelve hours because she'd asked him to. "Thanks, Matt. I know he's in good hands."

Matt nodded briefly and pushed the bed containing her father through the doors and into surgery.

Rose never generally thought about the essential ghastliness of hospitals. She'd worked around and in them so long that she'd become immune to the smell of sickness and disinfectants. The people who came into hospitals, with their life-threatening illnesses and terrible accidents, had families who loved them. She was reminded that a hospital was a scary place where not everybody made it out alive.

Jack had refused to call Daphne on the grounds that he didn't want to worry her, and he'd ordered Rose not to call her either. But he didn't tell Rose that she couldn't call one of her siblings, so she got on the phone to Marguerite who lived right on the property with Daphne. Marguerite promised to bring their mother to the hospital right away. "How serious is this?" she had wanted to know.

"Honestly, I don't know. The pacemaker surgery is pretty routine. What's worrying me is what's going on with his heart that makes him need one."

Marguerite and Daphne were more than an hour's drive away. Rose began to pace. She knew pacing up and down was a waste of energy, but she couldn't sit still, she couldn't focus, all she could do was believe. She believed in Jack's core strength and stubbornness. She believed in Matt's surgical abilities.

The minutes creaked by as slow and rusty as old machinery. She walked to the window and stood looking out. It was dark. Her view was of the parking lot. Streetlamps illuminated puddles and she could see dimples on their surfaces where it was still raining. Every once in a while, a car or truck would drive into the lot, or drive out again. She wondered idly who these people were, who they were visiting.

She gave up after a while and went back to pacing.

"Rose!"

She turned to find her mother running towards her with her arms held out. Rose had never been so glad to see her mom. Even though she felt that she should be the one comforting Daphne and reassuring *her*, in truth, she felt like a frightened little girl inside and she needed her mother's arms around her.

"Any news?" her mom asked softly.

"Nothing yet. He's still in surgery, but it shouldn't be much longer."

Daphne had obviously been working on her pottery when she'd received Marguerite's call. Bits of clay clung to her old, faded sweatshirt and dotted her hair like cement dandruff.

Behind her was Marguerite. Rose felt that her sister was holding herself together with an effort. Which was exactly how she felt. They hugged, and her eyes widened as she saw James stride into the waiting room. He wore his uniform which added a tone of seriousness.

They stood there, in an awkward circle, the four of them.

Daphne said, "I don't understand. Jack said he wanted to surprise you and take you for dinner."

Rose had had time to think about this. She said, "he's had pain for days and who knows how long he's had other symptoms? I think he wanted to take me to dinner today because he was going to ask me what I thought was wrong with him."

Daphne nodded, looking both worried and frustrated at the same time. "That is so like your father. Is he having open-heart surgery?"

"No. The surgeon doesn't have to open up the chest cavity. A pacemaker basically resets the heart's electrical system so the heart beats properly."

"But why is his heart off its rhythm?"

She shook her head. "We don't know yet."

Daphne wrapped her arms around herself.

James asked, "Who wants coffee?" He glanced at his mom and Marguerite then said, "I'll see if I can scare up some herbal tea."

Knowing he needed something to do more than any of them needed anything to drink, she said, "The cafeteria stocks herbal tea. It will still be open."

"I'll help you," Marguerite said and the two of them headed out.

"Why don't we sit down?" she suggested to her mom.

Daphne nodded and took a seat on one of the black vinyl chairs. "I thought something was up," she said, the words bursting from her. "When I asked him he told me everything was fine. But I've been married to that man for nearly forty years. I knew everything was not fine.

54

Why didn't I forced him to tell me what was wrong?"
She gazed at Rose out of her big blue eyes.

"He's stubborn, Mom. I'm guessing he didn't want
to worry you."

"Well it didn't work. I am worried." Her words
wobbled at the end, and Rose felt the tremor of emotion
go right through her.

"Matt Vasilopolous is one of the best surgeons I've
ever worked with. Dad could not be in better hands."
And she was hanging on to the hope that being in the
best hands would be enough.

They didn't talk much after that. James and
Marguerite returned with four cups of herbal tea. Rose
noted that the tea came in china mugs and suspected that
even in emotional turmoil Marguerite had insisted on the
environmentally friendly option rather than opting for
cardboard takeout cups.

She was halfway through her tea when Matt pushed
through the doors and into the waiting room. She
jumped to her feet along with her mother and siblings.
Daphne rushed forward to meet the advancing surgeon.
"I'm Jack's wife," she said. "How is he?"

Matt glanced around, caught her eye and nodded
imperceptibly, and he said, "Mrs. Chance, your husband
has a brand new pacemaker. He's out of surgery and
resting."

"Oh thank God," her mom exclaimed and then put
her hands over her face and burst into tears.

"We're going to keep him in for a few days and do
some more tests. We need to figure out why this
happened." Marguerite was closest and she grabbed her
mother and hugged her.

"Thanks."

Matt headed towards Rose and she could see the lines of tiredness on his face. She reached out her hands for his.

"Thank you. Thank you for doing this."

He flashed a tired, somewhat crooked smile. "Anytime. Your dad's sleeping. But you can go and see him for a few minutes."

James spoke up. "We're very grateful." He held out his hand.

They shook hands and Matt said, "I'm guessing you're the brother who's a cop."

James grinned, "Uniform gave me away, huh?"

"Yeah."

Rose said, "I was hoping you could help Matt get into Fennimen's shooting range for a stag party he's organizing."

"For the guy who saved my dad's life? I can do better than that. I teach firearms. If you like, I'll give you guys a lesson. When I give a lesson, we get the entire place to ourselves."

Matt looked as excited as a guy who's been in surgery for fourteen hours can look. "That is awesome! Thanks."

Rose stood back and watched the male bonding taking place before her eyes. She had a feeling those two were going to like each other. Both worked hard at jobs involving saving lives, and both had a goofy side. She shook her head, glad to have a second to regroup.

When Matt had emerged from the operating room and she'd seen on his face that the news was good, all she'd wanted to do was to throw herself into his arms for a big, warm hug.

Rose had a real problem with that impulse.

One: She didn't do vulnerable.

Two: She didn't do doctors.

And there was no way she could deny that she was becoming dangerously attracted to the scruffy surgeon.

Daphne and James and Marguerite headed in to see Jack, but Rose waited. Matt had lines of fatigue around his eyes and she knew he'd pushed himself to his limit. Because she'd asked him to.

"Thank you," she said. "I had no right to ask you to stay."

He stood there for a moment as though searching for words. After glancing around to make sure they couldn't be overheard, he said, "I wouldn't let Ogilvie operate on my dog."

"I still had no right to ask you to stay."

"You're welcome." Then he touched her arm. "Go see your dad."

"And you go get some sleep."

Seven

SINCE THE MOMENT Jack had stumbled into her office doubled over in pain she'd felt anything but calm. The man she had called dad for all of her life was seriously ill. Rose did not belong in the Chance family. She'd known it since she was old enough to recognize what a princess was. All those stories, those fairy tales about princesses being snatched away from their real homes, or forced to work in slavery until their true status could be outed had always resonated with the tiny Rose.

She loved Jack and Daphne with all her heart but they'd embarrassed her for most of her life. She didn't even recall how she'd first learned about fashion, but she knew that by the time she was in grade school she was convinced she did not belong in a family where wearing second hand clothes was a point of pride. Recycling and respecting the earth's resources was honorable and good, but she'd longed for shiny, sparkly, new.

In their usual new-age way, Jack and Daphne had refused to tell their eleven kids which of them was adopted and which were their natural children. Jack, in particular, with his bitter memories of being a foster kid, never wanted their adopted children to feel like second-class citizens. Rose, of course, had been convinced she was adopted from the moment she was conscious of how different she was from them. She'd never felt like a second-class citizen. She felt special. Of course, one day she'd be reunited with her real family. By the time she was old enough to realize that there wasn't as much royalty in the world as Disney would have you believe, she'd become certain that one day she'd find the people who were just like her.

The deal was that the kids could ask about their real parentage when they were sixteen years old, but sixteen came and went and she didn't ask.

She'd watch families on TV, the fancy ones, or pass well-dressed, fashionable people on the street and think, I bet I'm related to them. It was fun to picture herself among people she felt an instant kinship with. She'd also seen how upset Iris had been when she'd met her birth parents and discovered she was a product of a very twisted relationship and, in fact, getting pregnant had been her birth mother's last ditch effort to trap her married lover. The reunion had been a disaster and Iris had discovered how contemptible her birth parents were.

So, Rose hung on to her fantasies and put off ever finding out the real story.

The older she got, the less her parentage mattered to her. But she hugged her special status to her. When Jack built yet another crooked wall in their rabbit warren of a house, she could smile, not worrying that his crackpot gene was in her DNA. When Daphne showed up in

Portland in thrift store jeans with a mismatched patch sewed on the knee, she comforted herself that her real mother wouldn't be seen dead looking like such a wreck. But she loved them and worried about Jack's health.

She and Daphne were sitting with Jack the next day. Daphne had spent the night in her spare room and she'd rescheduled as much of her day as she could. Matt strode in. "Morning, Jack. How are you feeling?"

"A little tired, but a whole lot better than I have for the past few days."

"Good. Well, we got your test results back. You've got something called hemochromatosis." He glanced at Rose. "Rose can explain it all to you, but basically, your body produces too much iron. The excess iron is stored in your organs, especially your liver, heart and pancreas. Over time, the iron poisons those organs. That's what happened to your heart."

Jack looked confused. "But how did I catch it? Is it like a virus?"

"No. It's hereditary, the most common genetic disease among Caucasians. It was your bad luck that you inherited two faulty genes. It's typical to show up later in life."

"Can it be cured?"

"It can be managed. Basically, you'll have blood drawn on a regular basis to keep the iron levels in check."

Matt checked Jack's incision while he was talking. He nodded and reattached the bandage. "Everything looks good."

Daphne said, "So, if it's hereditary?"

"All of you should get checked. Even if your children only have one gene, they can still be carriers. It's a good thing to know."

"Well, I don't need to be tested," Rose said, happy for about the millionth time about her mysterious parentage. "I'm adopted."

Jack and Daphne exchanged a glance.

"Honey–"

Jack interrupted. "We always said we wouldn't."

Daphne made a *tsk* sound. "That was before you turned out to have a genetic disorder." She turned to Rose. "Darling, you really need to get yourself checked."

Rose stared at Daphne, then at Jack, as the meaning of those words sank in.

She imagined this was how people felt when they suddenly discovered all their savings had gone in a bank crash. Stunned. Disbelieving. Bereft. "But I can't be yours. We don't have anything in common."

Daphne got up and put a hand on her shoulder. "I'm sorry, honey. I know you always dreamed of something better."

"I'm seriously your kid?"

It was Jack who answered, "Yes."

She wanted to jump out of her chair and flee. If she'd been a kid, that's what she would have done, but she was an adult. So, she said, "Okay, I'll get the genetic testing." And then she began processing the incredible news.

All her princess fantasies, and it turned out she'd been Daphne and Jack's kid all along.

* * *

DAPHNE SETTLED ON Rose's couch, a glass of white wine in one hand. They had just returned from the hospital and were waiting for the Indian food Rose had ordered for their dinner.

"The doctor says your father can go home tomorrow," Daphne said.

"I know. That's great. He's really doing well mom. The doctors wouldn't let him go home if he wasn't ready." She felt that she needed to reassure her mother since a frown of worry creased Daphne's forehead.

"Oh, I know. He's doing well, but all he can talk about is all these projects he has waiting at home. He's already talking about the early spring planting and he's been sketching ideas for a new garage. He wants to build it himself."

"He's adjusting to a pretty big shock. His heart's been damaged by a condition he didn't know he had. Once he gets back home, he'll settle down and he will rest. All he has to do is listen to his body."

"I'm sure you're right, I'm just worried. He's always been so healthy. He never gets sick. He always tells me he's like one of those stubborn weeds in the garden; he thrives in stony soil and neglect. It's going to kill him to have to slow down and see doctors regularly."

"I know."

At that moment, their food arrived. They settled at her dining table to eat, and Rose refilled their wineglasses.

"I'm sorry about the circumstances," Daphne said,

"but it's really nice to have a meal with only the two of us."

"It is." She nibbled on a piece of Tandoori chicken, then fluffed her Basmati rice with her fork. "Mom, can I talk to you about something?"

Daphne glanced up from the dish of dal. "Of course you can."

She put down her knife and fork and picked up her wine. Why she should feel nervous about this conversation, she had no idea, but she felt strangely confused. She didn't even know where to begin.

Finally, she said, "Why didn't you tell me I wasn't adopted?" There. It was out. The issue that had been bothering her since that surreal moment in the hospital when she'd discovered that these very nice people, the ones she'd always been grateful to for taking her in, were her real parents.

Daphne looked at her with blue eyes—blue eyes that were very like her own. Those eyes were kind and compassionate, because Daphne was both of those things. She was the kind of woman who took in children no one else wanted even as she went right along having her own kids and never bothering to tell the misguided offspring which were which.

"You know the rules. Any one of our children could ask about their parentage when they turned sixteen. We never offered any information before sixteen and if a child preferred not to know then we respected that. To Jack and me you are all our children, as loved and treasured as though we'd given birth to every one of you."

She'd heard versions of that speech all her life,

always deeply thankful that somewhere out there were people who were like her, not like the hemp-glad, impractical, overpopulated Chances. "But you knew I believed I was adopted."

Was that a touch of sadness in her mother's eyes? Too bad. A lie was a lie even if it was an unspoken one. "Of course I knew. But you never asked. And I stuck to the agreement we made with all of you."

"But—"

"You know why you never asked." Daphne reached across and touched her hand. "Most children are afraid of the trauma of discovering they were adopted. That the people who should have loved them most in the world gave them away. But in your case the opposite was true. You were terrified of finding out that you didn't belong to anyone else. That you were exactly where you belonged. There was no wicked fairy, or evil stepmother who separated you from your real family. We were your real family. It wasn't up to me to destroy your fantasy."

"But I'm nothing like you. You and Dad are compassionate, you'd rather save the planet than buy a decent pair of shoes."

"I don't care about fashion. That doesn't make me a saint. And you do care about fashion. That doesn't make you a bad person. You save lives. You're a healer."

"I went into medicine for the money."

"Doctors who only want the money usually go into obscure specialties or cosmetic surgery. You're in family medicine and your patients love you."

"How do you know?"

"The guest room is also your home office. I read some of the cards on your bulletin board, and you've got photos of a lot of new babies. I think you love your work."

"Doesn't mean I don't want to make money."

"Why shouldn't you make money?"

"If you were me you'd be with Doctors Without Borders and what little money you earned you'd give away."

"But I'm not you. I respect your choices. Darling, I'm so proud of you and all you've accomplished."

"But why am I so different from you and Jack? So driven?"

Daphne laughed. "I have a little theory about that."

"Do tell." Daphne loved new-age psychology and self-help books as much as Rose loved Italian clothes and French lingerie.

"A lot of kids try to live up to the expectations their parents have for them. In some families, those expectations are ridiculously high. In your case, you were living up to the expectations of a fantasy mother and father who, for as long as I can remember, were some kind of royalty."

"You make me sound insane."

"No. You were imaginative. You built an entire world view around all those outcast princess tales."

"The Grimm people should be sued."

"I used to worry about you being so hard on yourself."

"Most parents want their kids to be successful."

Again with that angelic smile. "We only ever wanted you to be happy. I can see your face now, so wrinkled with concentration you looked like an old woman reading books that were too advanced for you, working on Evan and Iris's homework, thinking about college entrance exams when most girls were playing with dolls."

She hadn't realized Daphne was paying such close attention. It was impossible to explain the drive she'd felt to prove she was somehow smarter and better read than anyone else her age. "I wanted to be ready," she said slowly, understanding her own drive for probably the first time. "I wanted to be ready, to prove that underneath the Cinderella rags—"

"Please, we never dressed you in rags."

"Hand-me-downs. To me that felt like the same thing."

Daphne put down her knife and fork. "We were so concerned with teaching you kids about sustainability and respecting the earth's resources."

"I know." But a new dress now and then would have meant a lot. Her mom had a husband in hospital and enough problems. Besides, making her feel bad wouldn't make any difference. There weren't any kids at home any more, and oddly, she didn't think any of the others had suffered from the lack of new clothes the way she had. So she was a shallow fashion victim. She gave a lot of money to good causes so she didn't have to feel guilty every time she slipped into a little something with an Italian name on it.

"I swear, I was the only mother I knew who had to beg their child to study less."

"I was pretty intense, wasn't I?"

"You got accepted into Stanford Medical School beating out fierce competition from all over the world, so maybe you needed to be that intense."

"Maybe."

Eight

THE NEXT DAY, Rose and her mom took the tram up the hill to the hospital. Rose had an hour before her first patient so she went in with Daphne to see Jack.

He was lying still, something she'd rarely ever seen him do in all the time she'd known him. He was always in motion, designing something, attempting to build, renovate, or fix. Or he was in the garden. Even when he talked on the phone, which wasn't often, he walked up and down while he talked.

So, to see him so still, his head turned to stare out the window, was rare. From his vantage point, she was fairly certain he could only see sky. He looked smaller and paler then he'd ever looked. "Morning sweetheart," Daphne said, walking toward the bed.

Jack turned his head and it seemed as though he'd slipped into a mask. Suddenly he was talking. Gesturing. Twitching even. "Good morning, Daphne. Rose, thanks for coming in. I know you're both busy. It's crazy for you to spend time cooped up in here. Just because I have to doesn't mean you should."

"Nonsense. What would I be doing at home?"

"And my office doesn't open for an hour."

"I was thinking about the garden. You know that field where we put the peas every year? I think we should try growing artichokes."

Rose was no gardener, but the only time she'd seen artichokes growing was in California when she'd pulled over at a roadside artichoke farm while driving down the coast near Monterey.

"Well, that's an interesting idea, darling," Daphne said in her long-suffering, here-we-go-again way. The man had so many ideas, why were they so rarely good ones? "I'm not sure I've ever seen artichokes growing in our part of Oregon."

"That's because people are sheep, Daphne. Everybody plants the same dull stuff year after year. Peas, beans, potatoes, tomatoes, squash—Boring!"

"But everyone in our family loves peas. Marguerite sells a lot of them, don't forget."

He waved a finger and wagged it in the air. "She'll make a lot more money off of artichokes because nobody else local has them."

She felt something that made her look toward the door, and Matt strode in. Before she could glance away he looked at her and she experienced a sizzle that leapt between them as jumpy and unwelcome as an electric shock. It only lasted a moment but the impact stunned her, then he was turning to her father. "Well, Jack, how's it going today?"

"Excellent, Matt. I was telling the girls about artichokes. Do you like them?"

"Steamed, with lots of butter. Some like

mayonnaise and to mess around with frying and grilling. Not me. I'm a purist."

"I agree."

Matt listened to Jack's heart. Nodded. "Your liver test results came back and things are looking good. The only damage seems to be to your heart and we can control that. What do you say? Ready to go home tomorrow?"

"More than ready. No offense, this is a fine place you're running here, but I miss my own bed and my wife."

"I miss him, too," Daphne said, reaching for her husband's hand. They were like the high school couple going steady, which would be cute if they hadn't been acting this way for nearly four decades.

Rose watched Matt chatting with her Dad and for some reason recalled barging into his shower like a crazy person asking him to install Jack's pacemaker. She recalled vividly what she'd been too stressed at the time to register.

Matt, wearing nothing but a towel, rivulets of water running down his torso. She might as well have had X-ray vision. Her eyes saw right through the creased scrubs and she saw the muscular chest, the chiseled abs. Holy hell, the man was cut.

More, she recalled the way he'd looked at her, how he'd instantly agreed to help her father. Because she'd asked him to.

As though he felt her staring at him he turned and their gazes connected. Once more she felt that whoosh. She had a terrible feeling she was starting to blush as though he'd read her thoughts and knew she was picturing him half naked, droplets of water clinging to his skin as though they never wanted to let go. She and Matt might have stayed like that for a millennium or two but luckily her mother broke in. "You know a lot about artichokes for a surgeon."

He blinked, turned back. Shrugged. "I grew up in the restaurant business. My folks are Greek and they sent us out to work in their friends' Greek restaurant when we were old enough to wash dishes and bus tables. When you're in the food business, you learn about things like the best way to serve an artichoke."

"I love Greek food," Daphne said.

"Then you should check out my brother's food truck. Rose, you should take your mom to Alexei's."

"I should. You're right. We've been so busy."

"Ooh, a food truck. I'd love that. Let's do it for dinner. Marguerite's coming up to visit Jack this afternoon and then we'll go eat some Greek food." Then, with breezy casualness, Daphne said, "Matt, you should join us."

"Mother. I'm sure Matt is busy." What was this crazed ex-hippy doing? Trying to set her up?

He shot her a sympathetic glance with a lot of teasing behind it. "Call me when you're going. If I've got a break I'll come with."

"Great."

When Matt was about to leave, Jack piped up. "You never thought about going into the restaurant business too?"

"Nope. The tips helped put me through med school though."

"Rose went to Stanford, you know," Daphne said.

Matt's eyebrows flew up. "Really? You went to Stanford?"

"And had the student loans to prove it."

Her mother and father had never been the matchmaking types. And now she knew why. They sucked at it.

"She was in the top ten percent of her class. She's always been very smart and hard working."

She rolled her gaze. "I also have good eyesight, clear skin and sturdy, child-bearing hips."

Matt was having trouble not laughing at her and the more he tried not to laugh the more she wanted to hit him.

"You're not on the auction block, Rose," her mother protested.

"That's good, Mom, because I don't think anyone in this room is looking to buy."

Matt didn't linger very long after that. Rose got the feeling that if he stayed much longer he was going to start laughing so hard he'd choke. Maybe with some help from her.

After he left, Daphne said, "What a gorgeous man. Is there something going on with you two?"

"Apart from you pimping me out to him you mean?"

"Oh, as if I'd do that. I felt something between you, that's all. He is such a refreshing change from your usual choice of man."

"First, he's not my man." She thought for a second about what her mother had said. "And second, he's exactly like my usual choice of man. He's successful, good-looking, age-appropriate. He seems exactly like my usual type, apart from a serious lack of personal grooming."

Daphne and Jack exchanged a glance. Daphne said, "I can't explain exactly—and don't take this the wrong way—but with Matt you get the sense of a real person. Your other men have always seemed so . . ."

Jack finished the sentence for her, "Distant."

"Yeah!" Daphne agreed. "I think I've been intimidated by every one of them."

"Wasn't one of them royalty?" Jack asked. "A British count or something?"

"No. The Italian was the count. The British guy was merely a Sir."

"Right," Jack said. "He was the one who looked at me like I was supposed to curtsy."

"Oh come on," Rose said. "It wasn't that bad."

"Sir Peter Buckingham," Jack announced sounding pleased with himself. "I remember the name because I figured they named the palace after him."

"Okay, you two. I have to go to work. Do not try to set me up with anyone else while I'm gone. Understood?"

"Have a good day, honey. Marguerite and I will meet you at your place when you get off work. Then we can walk over to the food trucks. Maybe we should go to Voodoo doughnuts for dessert. I say that every time I come to Portland and I never make it. If we go, we'll bring you back one, Jack, to celebrate getting out of hospital tomorrow."

Her mom had moved on to doughnuts. Rose hoped that also meant she was thinking about something other than matchmaking.

* * *

MATT DIDN'T CHUCKLE. He didn't snort, guffaw or so much as smirk. Not until he got out of Jack's room. Then he turned into an empty corridor and did all three. It wasn't like patients didn't try to set him up with their daughters. They did it all the time. But to have Dr. Vogue of all people offered to him by her well-meaning folks did have a certain comic appeal. They'd all but thrown in a few head of cattle and a set of steak knives if he'd promise to take their daughter off their hands.

He had to thank Rose's parents. If it hadn't been for Jack's medical condition, he wouldn't have seen the side of Rose that wasn't cool and perfect all the time.

When she'd come to him, begging for his help with her dad, she hadn't looked cool or perfect. She was a daughter determined to save her dad. Even though she'd told him that her parents weren't snooty bluebloods, he hadn't believed they'd be anything like Jack and Daphne, who were impossible not to like but about as sophisticated as a pair of Birkenstocks worn with hand-knitted socks. Then, having the pair of them not-so-subtly try to get him interested in Rose was the icing on the cake. Her mortified expression had been the best part.

He was still grinning when he hit the OR to deal with a torn lung.

The day was no better or worse than any other. He was heading out when his cellphone rang. He'd never believed for one second that Rose would call him to go to Alexei's food truck, but it was Rose's name on his call display.

73

"Matt Vasilopolous," he said.

"Matt, I'm so glad I caught you. It's Daphne Chance."

"Daphne? What are you doing with Rose's phone."

"Oh, well, Rose is in the bathroom freshening up and I know what she's like, she's so convinced you're too busy that she won't even ask you to join us. So I thought I'd call you myself. We'd love to have you join us for dinner. The least I can do is buy a spanakopita for the man who saved my husband's life."

"Totally not necessary, Daphne. I was only doing my job."

"Well, will you join us anyway? I'm sure we'll get better service if you come along."

Oh, it was too tempting. And besides, he was hungry. "You know, I haven't had decent Greek food in weeks. I'd love to join you. Tell Rose I'll meet you there."

"Say, thirty minutes?

"Perfect."

He hadn't eaten at his brother's place for a while, or even seen his bro for that matter. He had basketball later so it would be good to get some food in him. Naturally, watching Rose's mother embarrass her with her heavy-handed matchmaking was going to be an extra bonus.

And to think, he'd imagined her family as some snooty, cold-blooded Easterners. No wonder Rose had believed she was adopted.

Nine

MARGUERITE AND DAPHNE talked artichokes for the entire time it took them to walk to the food trucks. Naturally, Marguerite, who made her living off the organic produce they grew, including the peas, was less than thrilled with Jack's latest brainstorm. Daphne explained that if planning an artichoke garden helped their dad to heal, then she wasn't going to stop him. But she promised to try and distract him, which was usually easy to do. Though, of course, that would result in some other wacky idea.

Even though they'd decided to eat at Alexei's, she wanted them to walk around the entire pod of trucks for the fun of looking at all the different stalls selling everything from bubble tea to fish and chips.

They wandered the loose square of trucks and trailers. There was shawarma, kebabs, tacos, churros, Thai, Vietnamese, hot dogs, hamburgers, and Greek. Alexei's was decorated in blue and yellow, the lettering in that font that screamed Greek. He'd gone all-out with the Greek theme. Posters of the Parthenon, a few plastic

Greek statues, decorator plates and twinkly lights surrounded the opening. It was still early so there wasn't much business. A lone customer stood talking at the window when they approached.

He turned as they grew closer and she felt her stomach go into free fall when she recognized the sexiest surgeon who'd ever held a scalpel. Matt was not here by coincidence, she was certain. "Oh, mother, you didn't!"

"Of course, I invited Matt. I told you I was going to. I want to buy him dinner as a small thank you for saving your father's life."

"I really doubt he came down here for a seven buck souvlaki, mom."

"Really? Then I wonder what he did come down here for?" Daphne said, nudging her.

No doubt she'd been more humiliated in her life. There were all the times her parents had come to school events in their hemp and tie-dye, including the memorable period when Jack had decided to get one of his ears pierced and took to wearing any single earring if Daphne or one of his daughters lost one of a pair. But then, in truth, they'd fit in at her school more than she had, so the humiliation hadn't been that bad. Nothing like, oh, for instance, what she felt at this very moment, with Matt standing there, pretty much a pity date set up for her by her well-meaning mom. When he caught her gaze she knew he was enjoying every second of her discomfort and had easily read her mind.

Daphne, however, remained clueless. "Matt," she cried, rushing forward and giving him a hug. A hug! One of the top surgeons in Portland and she was throwing her arms around him as though he were an old friend returned from a Greenpeace expedition.

Matt didn't seem to mind. In fact, he hugged her back. "I'm glad you could make it," he said, as though he'd done the inviting instead of Daphne.

"I am so happy to be here and to try your brother's food. Rose absolutely raved about how good Alexei's is."

She and Marguerite had caught up by this time and he turned to the guy in the truck he'd been talking to.

"Alexei, this is Daphne Chance and her daughters. Rose is a colleague of mine. And that's Marguerite."

"Pleased to meet you," he said.

She glanced up at Alexei. She'd seen him before, but never really paid attention. He usually cooked in the back while a pretty young woman served at the front of the truck so she'd never caught a good look at him. She did so now and her jaw would have fallen if she didn't catch it in time.

The February light was starting to go dusky so he was highlighted by the light within his truck, framed by the twinkle lights. If Matt was a good-looking guy, and he was, his brother was beyond words. Alexei had eyes that were large and almond shaped, with lashes so thick that any woman she knew would kill for them. His jaw was square, his nose classical, his brow thoughtful, and unlike his big brother, he obviously cared enough about his appearance to shave daily and have his hair cut regularly by a professional stylist. There was a statue of Adonis perched on a shelf and she thought Matt's brother was the spitting image of the mythical hottie.

For a second, all three women stood staring and she

knew they were thinking the same thoughts. Matt said, "Alex is the ugly one in the family, but we're nice to him because he can cook." Most likely this reaction happened with every woman who ever got near the too-gorgeous-to-be-real Alexei.

Little brother seemed unfazed by their regard, probably because he'd received it all his life.

"Have you considered modeling?" Daphne finally asked.

Alexei shifted uncomfortably, but Matt roared with laughter. "He's been approached by agents, casting directors and modeling scouts since junior high."

Alexei shrugged. "I like to cook." As if that explained everything.

The menu was listed on the side of the shutter thing that would close when the truck did. She drew her mother and sister's attention to it. "I can personally recommend the souvlaki platter but I bet everything's good."

There was almost no seating anywhere, but a small metal table sat on the edge of the sidewalk in front of Alexei's place. Matt gestured to it. "Any chance you can join us for a few minutes?"

"Yeah, sure. Soon as I've cooked your food and Melissa gets back."

"She your helper?"

"Yep. She's off on a break." Rose wondered how Melissa got anything done with the most gorgeous man on earth sharing a truck with her.

Daphne and Marguerite perused the menu and Rose said, "I'm going to go ahead and have the lamb souvlaki platter."

"Make that two," Matt said.

"And I will have the lemon chicken with Greek salad," Daphne decided.

Marguerite turned at last. "Greek salad and spanakopita, please."

"Coming right up."

They all got cans of soda or iced tea and then claimed the small table before anyone else got any ideas.

A young woman in an apron over jeans entered the truck a couple of minutes later and soon she and Alexei emerged with four paper plates of food. Rose prayed silently that her mom wouldn't give Alexei a lecture on the wastefulness of paper plates, but luckily Daphne was on her best behavior.

"Now, let me pay for all of this so we don't forget."

Alexei put his hands in the air. "On the house. When my brother comes for dinner, it's always on the house." He shot them a grin that showed them that his teeth were as perfect as the rest of him. White and even and shiny. "That way, if I need surgery, he'll have to give it to me for free. I figure I get the better deal. It's like insurance."

"I'm not operating on you for free," Matt informed him.

"Come on, I come in to your hospital with my heart torn in two and you wouldn't fix me up?"

"Sure I would. If your insurance paid for it."

"I can see exactly what you two must have been like as young boys," Daphne said, too accustomed to the stupid fights of her own boys to take any of this seriously.

Besides, the food was too delicious to waste time on

a boy fight. "Oh, my, this is delicious," Daphne said. Of course, she'd have said it to be polite, but Rose knew her well enough to hear authentic pleasure in her tone.

Marguerite chewed her salad thoughtfully. After a moment, she said, "Where do you get your produce from?"

"And here she goes," Rose said, mostly under her breath.

Matt was sitting next to her, so close that their knees bumped, so he heard her words. "What do you mean?" he asked softly.

"She grows and sells organic produce. It's like a religion."

He popped a chunk of tomato, no doubt conventionally grown in Mexico, in his mouth and settled back. "This should be fun."

Alexei seemed surprised by the question. He was clearly on his own dinner break as he had a plate of food in front of him too. More of the chicken that Daphne was raving about. He ate quickly and efficiently and she imagined a life working in restaurants was to blame. "I have a supplier."

Marguerite nodded. She pushed her long, dark curls over her shoulder and leaned in. For a relatively laid back woman who lived a quiet life where a yoga class was sometimes the most action she saw in a day, the pushing forward and getting her hair out of the way was assertive. "This salad is very good. The dressing is simple and wonderful, but the flavors would be sublime with organic, locally-sourced produce."

Alexei seemed surprised to be challenged by a woman who'd accepted free food from him. "Do you have any idea how much that would cost?"

Marguerite smiled, a smile as deliberate and rich as the slow food movement. "I know exactly how much it would cost. I grow organic vegetables for a living."

"You're kidding."

"I never joke about business," she said, as though she were a Fortune 500 exec discussing a merger.

"Good. I never joke about business either."

"I can tell from tasting this that the tomatoes have travelled too far. They were picked before they were ripe. The cucumber could be crisper, and the olives—"

"The olives came all the way from a farm in Greece where my parents grew up."

Marguerite nodded. "I was going to say, and the olives save the salad. But imagine if every morsel of this salad was as outstanding as the olives. And the cheese, which I'm guessing is also an authentic feta?"

"Yeah. Made here, but to high standards."

Marguerite's eyes glowed with intensity. Rose doubted she even noticed any more that she was addressing Adonis. To her he was a restaurateur who needed to learn about produce. Daphne was sufficiently engaged in the organic, local food debate that Rose felt safe talking to Matt with no danger of being overheard. She turned to him. "I am so sorry that my mother corralled you into coming out with us tonight."

"Hey, it's no problem. I had to eat. I have basketball later and I don't think I ate lunch."

"You don't think you ate lunch?"

"Can't remember."

She nodded. "Busy day, huh?"

"Oh, yeah. I don't know why, but as soon as you get

one jammer needing a pacemaker or bypass surgery, you get half a dozen. Why is that?"

She shook her head. "It's the same with me. Why do all my female patients get pregnant the same month, which means they all give birth in a clump? Couldn't they space it out a little?"

"Where's the consideration for the medical professionals?" He stabbed a tomato and studied it on the end of his plastic fork. "You know, I used to like his salad. Now I will always wonder how far the tomato traveled and how good it would taste if your little sister had grown it with her own hands."

"She's normally quiet and easygoing, but get my sister on the subject of local, organic produce and she's like those people who stand on the sidewalk pushing their magazines at you."

His eyes crinkled in amusement and she felt again that pull of intimacy that she didn't want to feel. She dropped her gaze to her plate and stabbed a cucumber.

A group of young people who looked like college students hung around in a ragged circle in front of Alexei's truck talking in low voices. When a consensus had clearly been reached, they all shambled up to place their orders. Alexei got to his feet. "Gotta go. Great meeting you."

"You too."

He turned back suddenly and said to Marguerite, "You have an email or something? I'll see what I can do about the produce."

She beamed so bright her happiness was blinding. "Of course I do." She dug in her bag, a patchwork quilt affair made from recycled blue jeans. Like it wasn't retro enough, someone had embroidered a peace sign on the thing. She pulled out one of her business cards, printed on recycled paper stock, and handed it to Alexei.

"Cool, thanks," he said, then waved and jumped back into his truck.

"And I should go too," Matt said. "I'm playing basketball tonight."

"Well, I'm sorry I didn't get to buy you dinner," Daphne said, "But thanks again for taking such good care of Jack."

"My pleasure. He's an easy man to like." Matt shook her hand, waved to Marguerite, said "See you soon," to Rose, and strode off down the street.

"Well, wasn't that nice?" Daphne said. "Now, let's go find some coffee and dessert. And I'll bet somewhere in this town is a folk singer. It's our last night together and your father's getting out of hospital tomorrow. We should celebrate. Too bad Matt couldn't stay."

"Mom, he's a busy guy."

"He's single you know, and I definitely think he likes you."

She hadn't believed her mother could embarrass her any more today. "Oh, God, Mom! Tell me you didn't ask him if he's single." If she had there was no choice. Rose was going to have to pack her belongings, say goodbye to all her patients, and relocate.

"Of course I didn't ask him if he's single. I would never embarrass you." She put an arm around each of her daughters. "I asked the nurse who's been mostly looking after Jack. She said that as far as she knows he's single. And nurses always know everything."

Ten

"WHEN WE TALK about guns, the first thing we talk about is safety." James Chance stood before the two-dozen guys at Harvey's stag party. He'd really come through for them, taking them to a private outdoor gun range used mainly by law enforcement. The skies were the same muted gray as a gun barrel, but there was no rain in the forecast and the weather was warm for May. They'd driven up a twisting mountain road into the middle of nowhere. The shooting area was a long field divided into lanes. A series of targets hung at the end of the lanes, everything from a human outline, to pie plates and water-filled plastic bottles. There was a dirt hill behind the targets that would catch stray bullets.

Even out of uniform James had an air of command. Not that he was a particularly imposing guy; Matt suspected it was because this was his world and they were all novices. As tough as they all pretended to be, they were desk jockeys and professionals who hadn't spent a lot of time around guns. He felt a pull of tension and suspected every one of the men here experienced something similar. Except for James who was as comfortable with a firearm in his hand as Matt was with a scalpel.

They stood in a long, covered area, kind of like a front porch, and behind them was a small clubhouse. James went through safety first, with the thoroughness of a man who does not want to get shot by some idiot who's played too many video games and forgets he's using live ammo among real people.

"Now, listen up, because I don't want to have to arrest anybody for stupidity, and Matt over there doesn't want to spend his day off stitching you up. No one ever walks in front of a guy with a gun, and if you've got a loaded firearm your safety is on unless you are shooting. Are we clear?"

A chorus of 'Yeahs' answered him.

"Good." He'd brought along a couple of young guys to help out. They handed out noise-canceling earphones, and then James showed them how to load a Glock pistol. They went in groups and practiced shooting. Matt had expected to be good since he was accustomed to work that demanded fine hand-eye coordination. However, as he faced the outline of a body, his mind flashed to the many gunshot wounds he'd treated back when he was a surgical resident. He went for the pie plate instead, managing to whack it a couple good ones.

Next, James showed them how to load and shoot a .22 rifle. No one noticed, but while he was speaking, his helpers were re-setting the targets.

This time, they were creepy-looking zombies, and the ammo was something green that exploded on impact.

They were laughing like a bunch of boys when they all returned to the covered area. Harvey clapped Matt on the back. "Gotta hand it to you, bro. This was a great idea." And Matt knew that once again he'd performed excellently under pressure. He could have researched and brainstormed for weeks and not come up with a better stag than this one. Manly without involving strippers or anything else potentially embarrassing to a future politician—or a future anything, depending on where their various lives took them.

The beer crawl was an obvious stag choice, but different since he'd focused on local craft beers, and ending up at the Hedgeman was inspired. Okay, Rose Chance was the one who'd inspired him, but she'd been part of his pressured brilliance from the start.

He could still recall the cold snake of panic that had crawled down his spine as he'd tried to grab a germ of brilliance from his exhausted brain, and her cool scrutiny had only spurred him on not to make a fool of himself.

He owed Rose. Well, since he'd saved her dad's life he suspected they were more than even.

They were hanging out for a few minutes winding down from the shooting high when Harvey clapped him on the shoulder again. "We need to bring James along for the rest of the night."

"Great." Matt had the same idea, and James fit right in with the rest of them. Harvey called him over and invited him to join them for the pub-crawl.

James grinned when told he was now an honorary member of the stag. "I'm not one to turn down a beer."

So he jumped in the minibus with the rest of them.

Thanks again to Rose Chance, who'd given him the number once she was certain they didn't need the vehicle for the same day she'd booked it.

A pub-crawl was pretty much a pub-crawl, and after the first couple of beers Matt couldn't tell one hop from another. They tried wheat beers and IPAs and lagers. He'd figured out a route that allowed them to walk as much as possible. Though there was definitely weaving involved in the end. Not to mention some staggering. When they got to Hazel Nut's, he'd hit the beer-goggles stage. Not drunk, not by a long shot, but less restrained than he usually was. He felt it, accepted it, warned himself not to be an ass. A couple of Harvey's friends were already fighting for the role of biggest ass-hat of the night. He didn't think he'd be a contender.

Harvey might have been the groom, but he took it easy on the booze. No Facebook post was going to derail his career. James was way more of a regular guy away from the guns, but Matt could see that he was taking it easy, too. He might be off duty, but Matt got the strong impression that he was always vigilant.

Matt walked over and took a seat beside Rose's brother. "What do you think? Those two going to end up in the drunk tank tonight?" He gestured to Dave, who sold commercial real estate. Matt suspected he was also bipolar and used alcohol to self-medicate. Matt put up with him because he'd been Harvey's friend since childhood. He was currently having a loud-voiced discussion about peak oil with Dawson, who managed a car dealership. Since they'd run out of facts long ago, they were using tactics such as talking faster and louder than the other to attempt to win their arguments.

James studied the two for a minute. "Na-ah. Worst that will happen is we'll get the minibus to take them home."

Matt glanced at him with respect. "You could do that? Make them leave if they don't want to?"

James wasn't a large guy, and as Matt had suspected, away from the guns and out of uniform, he fit right in with the rest of them. But when he said, "Yes. I could," Matt had no problem believing that those two would be waking up with hangovers before they realized they'd been sent to bed.

"You're a good man to have around," he said, clinking beer glasses with his new friend.

James grinned briefly. "So are you. You saved my dad's life. How cool is that?"

"You save lives too," he said. "Without law and order, we'd all be in danger all the time."

James didn't argue or pretend not to agree. He said, "Here's to us. Saving lives, day and night." They toasted again and drank.

"So, your sister," he said without planning to. Damn, he needed to slow down on the beer.

James didn't seem shocked he'd asked. Probably every man who'd ever glimpsed Rose wanted to know all about her. "Yes. My sister." He didn't offer more, but his tone wasn't discouraging. So Matt plowed on, not even sure where he was going or what he wanted to know.

"She's a good doctor."

James leaned his back against the rough-hewn table. "I'm not surprised. Rose was always good at everything; if she wasn't good right away, she'd quit doing it."

"Really?"

"Oh, yeah. You could look up perfectionist in the dictionary and find her picture staring at you."

"Why's she single?"

James was watching Dave and Dawson get more and more into each other's faces. Harvey and some of the others were taking bets on who was going to win. So far the atmosphere was more joking than serious but James looked like he wasn't going to let it get out of hand. "Why is anyone single?"

Since he didn't say anything else Matt concluded that he was supposed to answer the question. "I don't know. Haven't met the right person? Too busy?"

"Yeah. I guess. Rose isn't big on sharing her innermost thoughts with her kid brother." He grimaced. "All I know is she has terrible taste in men."

"Really?"

"She likes them rich and unavailable. For some reason they're always dicks as well."

Interesting piece of information to tuck away. Not that he really cared, he was only passing the time.

"I always think her schedule makes it hard for her to have a normal relationship." Suddenly James turned his head so he was regarding Matt straight on. "How about you? You find that? Or are you with someone?"

Well, he'd started the conversation, it was only fair that James should ask him about his love life since he'd asked about Rose's. "You're right. It's tough to find time to devote to a relationship when you're building a career or a practice."

"So, you're single?"

Was little brother a matchmaker? He made a face. "I

have a friend. Not anything with a future, but it's convenient for both of us."

James nodded. "Another doc?"

He shook his head. Then paused before speaking. "Is this going to get back to Rose?"

"Yeah, that's what I like to do in my spare time. Repeat guy talk to my sisters."

He stretched his legs out before him. "Right. I take it back." He found he liked talking to James. Maybe it was because they'd both grown up in big families, but both had the ability to carry on a private conversation while still being part of the larger group. How to describe Cheryl? "She's divorced. Not interested in anything complicated. Older."

"Sounds perfect."

"Works for both of us. She travels a lot and I don't give her a hard time about not seeing her enough. I work a lot and she is equally understanding. We see each other when we can fit time into our schedules. It's understood but never articulated that when either of us meets someone or wants something different it ends with no hard feelings." When he described his arrangement out loud it sounded pretty cold. For some reason he felt stupid and wished he hadn't told James. He hardly ever told anyone.

"She your date for Harvey's wedding?"

He shook his head. "No." Strangely, it had never crossed his mind to invite Cheryl. They went out to movies and dinner but never socialized with each other's friends. In truth, they barely even went out for dinners and movies. Mainly, they'd meet, usually at Cheryl's place since his was always a mess, share a glass of wine and he'd spend the night.

They'd been doing this for more than a year. Was he starting to feel restless? Like he wanted something more?

"So why are you asking about my sister?" James wanted to know.

Good question. To which he didn't have an answer. "I don't know. I think she's interesting."

James sent him a strange look. "Interesting? That's how you'd describe Rose?"

Why did that sound like a trick question? "Yes. I mean, obviously she's gorgeous and brilliant, but she's got more going on underneath that she tries to hide. I find that interesting."

"Huh," was all James said, but he smiled to himself as though enjoying a private joke.

They ended the night at the Hedgeman. It was the last stop of the night and Harvey got a bit teary when he described meeting Theresa. Things had quieted down since James had arranged Dave and Dawson onto the minibus. Matt didn't think they'd even noticed they were the only ones getting on the bus until it was pulling away.

The bus would be back at the end of the night to pick up the remaining stag participants and then drive them all home.

They'd abandoned beer and someone—Matt vaguely thought it was a lawyer colleague of Harvey's—had ordered a bottle of scotch. Oh, boy. Harvey was slightly less careful than usual as he waved his glass around, the amber liquid sloshing. "She was right over there, remember Matt?"

"I do."

"Two hot girls sitting having a glass of wine at that table right there." He aimed his finger as though it were a gun, though in his current condition he couldn't have hit the side of a barn if he was inside the barn. "I thought she was cute, and she had this way of tossing her hair over her shoulder that made me think I had to get to know her."

"But you were too shy," Matt interjected, remembering the evening well.

"Not too shy. I was waiting for my moment."

"You'd still be waiting if I'd left it to you," he joked.

"So my best man here swaggered over to their table and next thing I knew, these two hot girls were sitting with us." Harvey blinked rapidly. "I think it was love at first sight."

"How did you know? How did you know that she was the one?" Even though Matt had been present he didn't witness any fireworks, no sign from above. Harvey had done his Harvey thing, impressing the girl to the best of his ability, and she'd pretended to be impressed. He thought Theresa was a nice woman, pretty but not a great beauty. Why, out of all the single women out there, should she be the one? Why not her equally fun and attractive friend?

Or why would Harvey be the one for her? It was a mystery. He felt that there should be more choice in the matter of who a man fell in love with. After all, he was going to be stuck with her for a long time. It would be nice if he had a bit more control. But, according to Harvey and all the love songs, the movies, the plays and ballets, love was like a particularly nasty virus. You caught it and there wasn't much you could do but ride it out.

"You're a lucky man," James said, raising his own glass of scotch.

"You're coming to the wedding," Harvey announced.

James looked more horrified than gratified at the invite. "No. Really, it's fine. Happy to join the stag."

"No, I mean it. You're a good guy. Gonna be one of my inner circle, isn't he Matt?"

"Harvey talks like he's already the President when he's pissed," Matt explained. "There is no inner circle."

Harvey snorted. "You don't see it because you're in it. James is one of us. Knew it when he got rid of Dave and Dawson so elegantly." The word elegantly got tangled with the scotch, but Matt didn't think he'd have managed any better. He was keeping his words to no more than two syllables to be on the safe side.

When the scotch bottle was empty, he was about to call the bus when two of the younger guys ordered a round of shots, James and Matt exchanged glances. He shrugged and put his phone away. An hour later, the ragged group staggered to the minibus. He reached the door, glanced back at the bar. He did not want to get on that bus and go home.

He said, "You guys go on. I have to do something."

"You gotta take a leak? We can wait," Harvey said.

"No. Have to make a call."

James wasn't in great shape, but he was better than the rest. "You need me to wait for you? We can grab a cab."

He shook his head. "Private call."

James grinned. "Tell Cheryl, 'hi'."

He watched them climb aboard the bus and saw the orange signal light flash before the minibus pulled out into traffic.

He headed back inside the bar, settled at a table in a dim corner.

Squinted at his phone. Pushed a button.

Eleven

ROSE'S EYES FLEW open as a shrill noise pulled her out of sleep. The phone. Right. Her heart banged against her ribs, her first thought being that her father had become ill again.

She grabbed up her phone and the panic increased when she saw it was Matt calling.

"Matt? What is it?" Please, please let her father be okay.

"I was just thinking about you. Wanted to thank you for the minibus. And your brother. Thanks for your brother. He's a good guy."

In the few seconds it took her to realize that Matt was calling her from a bar and was not sober, her heartbeat went back to normal as relief flooded her. Her dad was fine. Matt she wasn't so sure about.

"You're welcome for my brother. And yes, he is a good guy."

"I'm sitting here thinking about love at first sight."

"Oh, you really are drunk." Of course. The stag was tonight.

"In vino veritas," he said grandly. She wondered if that was accurate. Was a drunk more likely to tell the truth?

"What is this truth you want to tell me?" She could hear the noises of a rocking bar in the background.

"Do you believe in it? Love at first sight?"

She pulled her knees up to her chest and settled back against her pillows. "No. I don't. Do you?"

"See? That's another thing we have in common." She had no idea what the first one was. "We're both scientists. Don't believe in that hocus pocus."

"Where are you?"

"The Hedgeman. This is where Harvey fell in love at first sight. I'm sitting at the table where it happened."

"Is the stag still going on?"

"Nope. They all left. But I told them to go on. I needed to call you."

She was amused but also filled with dread that his drunk dialing was going to put their budding friendship back into awkward territory.

"I think you should call me tomorrow when your head is clearer."

"Come down and have a drink with me."

"That's why you called me?" She didn't bother telling him how late it was. He wasn't going to take in details in his condition.

"Minibus is gone. Guys are all gone home. No one will ever know."

Even though he'd woken her, he was kind of cute when he was drunk. "You want to have a secret drink with me?"

"Didn't put that well. Come on, I need to talk to

you."

"What about?"

"I told you. Love."

She could hang up and let him find his own way home, but he had saved her dad's life. He'd gone back on shift because she'd asked him to. The least she could do was to drive him home and make sure he got inside safely.

"Okay. Wait there. I'm coming."

"Excellent. What do you want to drink? I'll order it."

She rolled her eyes. "Let me choose something when I get there."

She dressed rapidly in jeans and a sweater, pushed a comb through her hair and brushed her teeth. Maybe she was picking up an inebriated friend downtown, but nothing would induce Rose to leave her apartment without a swipe of lipstick and another of mascara.

Driving downtown late on a Saturday night required all her wits. There were drunks ambling into the road, kids with nothing better to do hanging around smoking, cabs darting in and out of traffic, red lights, one-way streets. By the time she'd found parking, she was completely wired as though she'd drunk four cups of strong coffee.

When she walked into the bar she saw that it was still hopping. How anyone could fall in love here, of all places, was incredible. The music was too loud to talk, the dance floor was crowded and it was dark enough that your best friend could be on the premises and you wouldn't see them.

She saw Matt, though, right away. He was sitting

alone at a table for two. He had a half glass of something that looked like scotch in front of him. He was staring into it as though the theory of everything was written on the surface of the liquid. Something about his air of—what? Sadness? Confusion? It got to her.

She stepped forward. "Hi, Matt," she said softly.

His face lit up when he saw her. "You came."

"Yes. I came."

"Sit down. Have a drink."

"I think I'll take a rain check on the drink. How about I drive you home."

He squinted at her. "Do you know where I live?" He wasn't incoherent, falling-down drunk, but she noticed he chose words with care and his gaze was slightly unfocused.

"No. Do you think you can direct me?"

He thought about it seriously. "Yes."

She caught the eye of a waitress. "Is his tab paid up?"

The young woman in the short black dress grinned. "Oh, yeah. And he's a very generous tipper."

"Good. Okay, pal. Let's get you home."

He got to his feet and walked pretty steadily for a man in his condition, to her car.

He dodged around a light pole. "I'm not drunk, you know," he announced.

"Good to know."

The night was chilly but he didn't seem to notice. "Why don't we?"

She shot him a glance. His hair was flopping over his forehead in unruly curls. Why did she want to reach over and smooth them back? His eyelashes were ridiculously thick and curly. The pub-crawl hadn't improved his general air of slovenliness. There was something sexy about him, though, with his stubbled cheeks and his I-could-eat-you-all-up white teeth.

"Pretty sure I don't want to answer that."

He turned to her, and the intensity in his gaze pulled at her. "Why don't we believe in love at first sight?"

She doubted he'd remember this conversation in the morning so she tried to answer honestly. "I've seen it happen to other people. I think love at first sight exists. I don't believe in it for myself."

She got him into her car and helped him with his seatbelt.

"Love is a pain in the ass. Like a virus." He peered out the window ahead. "Or the IRS."

She imagined that somewhere inside his inebriated brain comparing love to the IRS made sense. "Where do you live?" She wondered if she'd have to dig out his wallet and consult his driver's license to get his address but he told her. He lived in a house in the Pearl District.

As they headed to his place, she wondered what had made him ditch the rest of the stag participants instead of riding home on the minibus.

"Pull over here," he directed. She found herself in front of a craftsman cottage that begged for a rocker on the front porch and pots of winter pansies. If she'd thought at all about where he'd lived she'd have pictured him in a modern condo, something like hers, not in a turn-of-the-century cottage.

She pulled over and he turned to her as though continuing a conversation she thought they'd dropped. "Yeah. That's the thing. Harvey was sitting there tonight gushing about Theresa and how he fell in love with her at first sight. Even though it was kind of sick making, he believed it."

"Do you?" He seemed tortured by this notion.

He turned and their gazes connected. She felt a searing connection, somehow stronger now he didn't have his usual barriers up. She watched his face scrunch. "I don't want to."

She couldn't stop the laugh that burst out of her. "Then don't."

"It's like not believing in terrorism. Or earthquakes. Not believing doesn't stop them happening."

The engine purred quietly as she'd left the car running but he didn't seem in a big hurry to leave. She thought about what he'd said, in vino veritas. Maybe, for him, a lot of beer followed by scotch was like truth serum. Maybe she could ask him anything and he'd have to tell her the truth. She said, "You called me an interesting woman."

He shot her a glance. "Says who?"

"Theresa. She told me when we were shopping for bridesmaid dresses. When she discovered we know each other, she asked you about me and you said you thought I was an interesting woman."

He might be drunk but he wasn't stupid. "You sound pissed."

"I'm not. I was . . . surprised, that's all. It's a funny thing to say about someone you work with. Makes it seem like you don't like me very much."

His mouth twisted. "Oh, I like you fine." He shrugged. "But Theresa seems to have gone into the matchmaking business. She's a nice lady but she's got a big mouth and too much energy and I do not want her interfering in my life. I probably said that to throw her off."

"So, you don't think I'm interesting?"

He unclipped his seatbelt, turned to her. "I do think you're interesting, but it's not the first word I think of when I think about you."

Okay, now would be a good time to back off from interrogating him. He had an intensity about him that made her realize just how small the interior of her car was and how much of the space he seemed to fill. She wanted to say something cool and smart to him, but she couldn't think of anything cool and smart. Her words came out husky when she asked, "What is the first word you'd come up with to describe me?"

She saw a man who appealed to her in a deep, elemental way, staring at her mouth so intently her lips tingled. He said, in a low, slow voice that mesmerized her, "When I think of you, the first word that comes to mind is irresistible." He leaned toward her, clearly telegraphing that he was planning to kiss her. She had plenty of time to stop him but for some reason she didn't. Instead, she leaned into him and met him half way. The kiss was like him: sexy, unrestrained, not polite or groomed, but raw. Oh, my, was it raw.

He didn't offer.

He took.

He didn't ask.

He helped himself.

He didn't ease her into the kiss.

He plunged ahead.

He didn't tease a response out of her.

He forced one.

When he finally pulled away, she felt herself trembling, which seriously irked her.

He might be inebriated, but this man knew exactly what he was doing, and what he was doing to her. He resettled himself slowly. "Nice," he said. His eyes were an open invitation for more. "Do you want to come in? Make sure I get to bed okay?"

And she was so tempted she wanted to slap herself. She wasn't drunk. What was her excuse? "Some other time. Goodnight," she replied.

A glint of humor crossed his eyes, big, dark eyes with mesmerizing flecks of gold embedded like hidden treasure you had to search for.

"Goodnight. And thank you for the ride."

"You're welcome," she said, as prim as a Sunday school teacher.

Of course, she couldn't help him into his home or heaven only knew what would happen, but she watched him all the way to the door. She made sure he got inside okay, and then pulled away from the curb fervently hoping that by tomorrow he'd have forgotten all about their steamy kiss.

She only wished that she could forget that kiss. But as she drove, she could still taste him. The scotch, definitely a hint of beer. And was she crazy or was that a note of hazelnut?

Twelve

ROSE WAS JOGGING beside the river at Waterfront park the next morning, heading toward the Steel bridge when James's call came in. It was a glorious day, sunny and warm enough to be outside, but not too warm. Perfect jogging weather. She'd worked up to a nice rhythm and was pounding along happily, refusing to let her mind veer to the strange incidents of the night before, the call from Matt and the searing kiss.

The only reason she had her phone with her was because she'd downloaded an app that tracked her mileage and speed and let her compete against herself. She always tried to run a little faster, a little further, as though she could outrun herself.

Most calls she'd let go to voice mail. Not this one. She slowed to a stop and answered. "Hey, bro."

"Sis. How's it going?"

"Good. You sound remarkably cheerful for a man who was on a pub-crawl until the wee hours last night."

"How do you know we were out until the wee hours?"

Damn. Trust a detective to figure out she had knowledge she shouldn't possess. "I assumed you would be. That's why I told the minibus driver to be prepared to put in some overtime." That sounded reasonable and was also true.

James clearly found it reasonable too, for he said, "Yeah. We went way later than I thought."

"You sound good, though. Cheerful even. I bet a few of the boys aren't feeling so good this morning." One in particular she could think of.

"Ah, boys have to let loose sometimes. It was a good group, though. Glad I went."

He had to be calling her for some reason. "Any good gossip you want to share?"

There was a tiny pause and she thought, aha, he has something, but he said, "Nah. Can't break the guy code."

She rolled her eyes. "You mean you can't remember a thing."

He laughed. "When did you turn into a prude? Speaking of which, what did I interrupt you from? Hot sex? You're panting."

Her imagination immediately flashed to an image of her and Matt, naked and entwined. She snapped the image shut as though clicking out of a porn site she'd accidentally stumbled onto on her laptop. "If I were having hot sex would I answer the phone?"

"Depends who was calling."

She laughed again. "Such an egotist. As a matter of fact, I'm running." She checked the stats on her app and grimaced. "Scratch that. I'm jogging. Slowly." A couple of chatting moms jogged by pushing strollers, no doubt going twice the speed she'd managed. She really needed to get back to a more regular fitness schedule. A couple walking a dog whose short little legs could barely keep up with them came toward her.

"I called to see if you have a date to Harvey's wedding."

"It's not the high school prom, James. A woman doesn't have to have a date."

She could hear his smile. "So, that's a no, then."

"That would be a no. I'm in the wedding party, so I'd end up dumping my date most of the time anyway." And why was she explaining her dateless state to her little brother exactly?

"I was thinking I could be your date."

"You're going to Theresa and Harvey's wedding?" Like all of them, James guarded his free time. Why would he want to go to the wedding of people he barely knew?

"Thinking about it. Harvey asked me last night. He's a good guy. Might want to get to know him better. And I didn't really know Theresa growing up but we're from the same town. Plus, I can drive you home after."

"I was going to call a cab to get home. But, sure. Thanks. If you end up going, you've got a date." She was happy to think she could get a ride home with her brother, but had to wonder if the real attraction to the wedding was one very pretty, very waif-like bridesmaid.

She ended the call and rolled her shoulders. She had one week until the wedding and she was determined to fit into her dress in the most flattering way possible.

"Okay, running app, I am going to kick your butt," she promised, putting her ear buds in once more and pounding off down the path.

* * *

ROSE HAD NO reason to go to Pacific Crest hospital. She had no patients having babies or surgery. This was a good thing, she decided. She got on with her work. The work of ear infections, bladder infections, skin infections, eye infections, flu bugs, car accidents, pregnancies, and all the bumps and bruises of life. A few of her patients insisted on searching out their symptoms online and diagnosing themselves with everything from advanced cancer to Parkinson's disease. Fortunately, her advanced cancer case turned out to be heartburn and instead of Parkinson's, her elderly patient was suffering from anxiety since her only son had lost his job.

She prescribed, she soothed, she counseled, and listened. So much of medicine was listening. Sometimes she took the place of family members who didn't have time, sometimes she felt she filled the role that ministers did for the more religious.

Most of the time, she loved her work, especially when the visit was a happy one.

"Belinda," she cried, smiling warmly as she entered her examining room to find her newest patient, Pippin Tate, sucking happily on her fingers having no idea she was here for her first check-up. "How are you feeling?"

"Good. I'm good. More tired than with any of the others, but Pippin's such a good girl, aren't you, baby?" she asked in the sing-song voice of a mother to her infant. Pippin picked up on the tone and turned her head to her mother's voice. Which meant baby's hearing was excellent and she was bonding.

"That's good. You both had a rough start. I'm glad she's a good baby."

"Here, I brought you something," Belinda said. "It's a bottle of our homemade cider."

"Thank you." Rose often received small gifts like this, bottles of homemade wine, pickles, various preserves, sometimes a box of chocolates or scented soap.

She accepted the bottle and placed it on her desk. Then she examined both mother and baby, pronouncing both healthy and thriving.

She left her office at the end of the day and walked to her car. She slowed her steps as she approached. A man was leaning against the hood. A man she recognized.

"Matt," she said. "What are you doing here?"

"I want to talk to you."

"You could have come into my office." He also could have called first.

"Didn't want to bother you. I remembered your car."

"Okay."

She stood and waited, figuring he'd accosted her for a reason. She hadn't seen him since she'd driven him home from the stag and she forced herself not to think about how his lips had felt on hers.

He shifted. He was wearing jeans, boots that seemed more appropriate for hiking than street wear, and a dark blue shirt open at the neck that would have looked better for an iron. He needed a shave and his hair was its usual mess. "You haven't been in the hospital."

"No, I haven't. My patients are all between births and nobody's needed admitting. It's been quiet."

He rolled a pebble with the toe of his boot. "I wanted to talk to you."

She began to feel amused at his obvious discomfort. He was always so cool and together, a man in control of life and death, so it was kind of cute to watch him squirm because he'd got drunk and made a fool of himself in front of her. "Okay."

"Look, about the other night, I shouldn't have called you."

She'd been dreading this first encounter, certain she'd feel foolish and awkward since that steamy kiss, but now that he was so obviously feeling foolish and awkward himself, she was able to enjoy the moment. She opened her eyes wide. "Is that what you're apologizing for? Drunk dialing me?"

"It was late." He rolled the pebble the other way beneath his boot, all his attention focused on it. "Sometimes I think the cellphone is the worst invention ever. It's too easy to call people when you shouldn't be calling at all."

"Yeah. That speed dial, definitely invented by the devil."

"My thoughts exactly."

"So? You're here to apologize for calling me so late?"

"And for asking you for a ride home. I was stupid. Should have called a cab. You were probably asleep." Now he was making a circle with the stone under his shoe.

"I was. Asleep, I mean."

His gaze shot to hers and she felt a sear of heat before he dropped it to somewhere around her navel. "I might have been out of line."

"Out of line? In what way?" She had no idea why she was poking at him like this. Why couldn't she let it go and accept the fumbled apology he was trying to make?

He glanced up and she really wished she hadn't poked at him. The awkwardness was gone and she felt all the assurance of a man who knows his own power. He pushed himself off the car and took the single step it took to bring his body within touching distance of hers. She could feel the heat coming off him, practically smell his skin.

"I should have got on the bus with everybody else. I'm sorry I called you so late and asked you to pick me up." She didn't say anything so he waited a second and continued. "Thanks for driving me home."

"You're welcome."

He sighed. "You're not going to make this easy for me, are you?"

"Make what easy?"

She felt he was more amused than sorry. His gaze settled on her mouth. "I think I might have kissed you."

Her lips tingled under his gaze. "You *think* you might have kissed me?"

He stepped even closer. If she weren't a woman of strong backbone she'd have taken a step back. Because she didn't move their bodies ended up a whisper away from touching. She had to tip her chin up to look him in the eye. "My memory's a little fuzzy. Since I was inebriated at the time. I can't be sure whether it was a fantasy or reality."

"Do you often kiss me in your fantasies?"

She realized her mistake when his lips quirked. "You have no idea what we do in my fantasies."

No. Her pulse was not kicking up. No, her blood was not racing. She was not so easy to seduce. The silence lengthened. She could answer in a way that would let him know she was interested, or she could back the hell away. For a second she wasn't sure which way she wanted this to go, and then the decision was taken out of her hands. His cell phone rang.

He checked the call display and made a face. "Dr. Vasilopolous," he snapped. He listened for a moment, then checked his watch. "I'll be there in fifteen."

He snapped his phone shut. "I'm on call," he told her. "Have to go." He let his gaze smolder on hers for only a moment. "But this is not over."

As she got into her car she reminded herself that what had just happened was exactly the reason that she didn't date other medical professionals. She'd fully intended to make it clear to Matt that she wasn't interested. But she would have liked to do it in her own time, not have the hospital do it for her.

Thirteen

WHILE MATT CUT and patched and spliced, he was aware of a vague sense of annoyance in the back of his mind, like the hum of a faulty appliance. He could ignore it for a while but the hum wasn't going away until he fixed the problem.

After Wednesday night basketball, he usually showered and cleaned himself up a bit before heading to Cheryl's place. She'd arrived back a couple of days ago from a two-week trip to Barcelona. This would be the first time they'd seen each other since she'd left. He drove over to her place, a high-end townhouse that boasted top-of-the-line everything. She let him in, kissed him lightly on the lips. "I poured us some wine," she said, walking ahead of him into her living room.

The gas fire flickered over her collection of modern art. Cheryl had a passion for art and a good eye. She consulted for a few galleries. "How was Spain?" he asked, accepting a glass of red wine.

"Fine. Busier than I expected. The weather was warm." She crossed to sit beside him on the sofa, reached for him. "But I don't want to talk about Spain." She kissed him.

He let her kiss him and then he pulled slowly away. She raised her head and, while she didn't say anything, her eyebrows rose in a silent question.

Damn it, damn it, damn it! He drew in a slow breath, faced the inevitable. "I think I might have met someone," he said.

She picked up her wine glass and sipped. "You think you might have met someone? You don't sound too sure."

He tried to smile but he felt as foolish as he must sound. "I've definitely met someone. In fact, I've known her for a while. But I've become . . . interested."

"All right. And is this other person interested in you?"

And wasn't that the question. He leaned back, staring at something that looked very much like a Picasso and probably was. All angles and confusion, a woman with part of her face under her clavicle and another part where her belly ought to be. He slumped back against the couch. "Yes." He turned to regard another of Cheryl's paintings. This one as natural as a photograph, a woman in an evening gown staring back over her shoulder, smirking as though she knew more than the viewer. Certainly more than Matt did. "Maybe." Then he let out a breath. "The truth is I'm not sure."

Cheryl nodded. "And you don't want to continue this," she gestured from him to her and back again, "because you want to pursue this woman who may or may not be interested?"

"Yes."

She didn't chuck her wine in his face or act hurt. She was as cool as she'd always been. "Well, I will be sorry to see you go, but we always knew this day would come."

He nodded, feeling a rush of sadness. "Still be friends?"

She wrinkled her nose. "I wish you well, Matt, I really do, but neither of us has time for more friends. I think maybe we're done."

He nodded slowly. She was right, of course. But damn, he felt set adrift. They chatted a while longer, but Cheryl was right. Their relationship had always been simple and uncomplicated, the end clear.

But, as he walked back out of her townhouse an hour after he entered it, he wondered what the hell had just happened. He'd had no intention of ending things. Not until Cheryl had kissed him and he'd known she wasn't the woman he wanted to kiss.

Trouble was, the woman he was pretty sure he wanted didn't seem to feel the same way about him.

As he headed home, he contemplated calling Rose. In fact, he had his cell phone out and her number staring at him when he put it away again. He didn't think he'd made the greatest impression on her recently.

Well, apart from that saving her dad's life thing, but he didn't want to have to play that card to get her to see him. That would be pathetic. In his relationships with women he'd never had to stoop to pathetic, and he wasn't about to start now.

What he needed was a plan.

Or maybe advice from the coolest woman he knew: his mom.

It wasn't too late so he called home.

His mom answered and as soon as he'd identified himself, asked, "Is everything all right?"

"Yes, mom, everything's all right. I almost hate to call you because every time I do you think something bad's happened."

"No," she replied firmly. "I like to ask about trouble immediately so I know if anything terrible has happened. Now I know it hasn't and I can relax." His folks had been in America for nearly forty years but they still had pretty strong accents. Mostly because they spoke Greek to each other and most of their friends were Greek. Since they'd been determined their kids would assimilate they'd always spoken English at home when the children were around but now everyone had moved out, phoning home was like calling Athens. His conversation with his mother was half English half Greek. He'd been doing this for so long that he never even noticed when they switched from one language to another.

"So, how are you?"

"I'm fine."

"Are you eating properly?" Since eating properly to his mother meant meals at regular times with many courses, taken in the company of big groups of people, she'd stage a Greek intervention if he knew how many meals he grabbed on the fly. Sometimes he couldn't remember if he'd eaten sushi, a burger or nothing at all when he finished his shift. He pretty much based meals on whether he was hungry or not.

He sidestepped the question by saying, "I'm healthy."

His mother was not fooled. She made a snorting sound. "You should get married. A wife and a family would make you slow down. And you'd eat."

"I'm not even the oldest," he complained, not that her telling him to get married was a surprise. In fact, she was right on schedule. Her questions had a rhythm as predictable as the tide. *Is everything all right? Are you eating? Why aren't you married?* He smiled, hearing Greek music playing in the background, as well as the TV where his dad had one of his favorite cop shows turned up full blast. "I love you, Ma."

"I love you too, Mattius. So, you're homesick. I'm not surprised, living out there with all the rain."

"Do I have to be homesick to call my favorite girl in all the world?"

She laughed, "And I shouldn't be your favorite girl in the world. I can't give myself grandchildren!"

Not even going there. "I do like someone," he admitted.

"It's about time!" Then she raised her voice and yelled to his dad, "Patros, Mattius has a girlfriend."

"No. Ma. I don't have a girlfriend. I like her. I didn't say she likes me."

"What's wrong with her? Is she blind?"

"He's dating a blind girl?" he heard his dad yell, closer now so he'd obviously come into the kitchen where his mom was. "That explains it."

He heard the thud and *oof* as his mom smacked his dad. He felt as though he were sitting there with them in that kitchen. He should take a trip back there when he next got some vacation. They were crazy, loud, interfering and he loved them like crazy. "She's not

115

blind, she's busy, I guess."

"Is she interested in you?" his mom wanted to know.

"Yes, I think so. But she's another doctor. And she never goes out with doctors."

"That's funny, because neither do you."

"So, what do I do? Drop it because we both have crazy schedules?"

"Is she young enough to give me grandchildren?"

He winced. It had been such a bad idea to call his mom. "She's young enough, but my guess is probably not. I don't think she wants kids."

She sighed. Muttered in Greek. "Good thing I had five kids. One of you better give me grandbabies."

"Is that all you can think about?"

"No. I can think about lots of things at once. I can think about grandbabies and I can think that all I want is for you to be happy. Will she make you happy?"

"I haven't even had a date with her yet. Not dinner, or a movie. I don't even know why I'm talking about this."

"Why don't you ask her out? Ask her to dinner? Too bad your brother Alexei only has trucks. But there must be one decent restaurant in Portland. Ask your brother, he'll know."

Since a good restaurant could only be a Greek one, he didn't argue that Portland had great restaurants. He promised to ask his brother for a recommendation. He also chose not to mention that Alexei had met Rose. He preferred not to think of his mother and brother discussing his problematic love life behind his back.

"We're going to be at the same wedding this

weekend."

"Good. That's good. Will she bring a date?"

"I don't know. I don't think she's seeing anyone."

"Then that's your chance. Weddings always make a woman feel romantic." Then she turned on the mom voice. "When was the last time you had your hair cut?" She didn't even wait for him to answer. "You get your hair cut. Get a barber to give you a proper shave so you don't get all swarthy and Greek by noon."

"Swarthy and Greek? Women love that."

"Not all of them. And make sure your shoes are polished. You're as handsome as Adonis, but you don't try. Put some effort into how you look. She'll notice. She'll appreciate."

"How will she know I did it for her?"

More muttering in Greek. "She's a woman. Trust me, she'll know."

"Okay. Good talking to you, Ma. Love to Dad."

"Call me next week and tell me how it went."

"I will."

"And bring her home with you so we can meet her."

"Ma, we haven't even had a date yet." He could not even imagine how Rose would feel being hauled in to meet his crazy family. Then he recalled how embarrassed she'd been by her mom and dad doing a big sales job about her for his benefit and he thought he knew exactly how she'd feel when his folks pushed him at her.

"Well, when you've had a few dates, then bring her around."

"Love you.

"Love you back."

His mother was from a different generation, a different continent, a different culture. But he still dropped his good shoes off to be polished, his tux to be pressed, and made an appointment at the salon Harvey patronized. They could do his hair and shave him the morning of the wedding.

Then he tried to forget about Rose Chance and concentrate on the million other things he had to do.

His mom was right. He never dated other medical professionals. Too confusing, too chaotic.

But he'd never met another medical professional like Rose Chance before.

He kept things casual in his private life for a reason. He didn't have the time or energy to devote to a serious relationship. That's why Cheryl had been so perfect for him. And now he'd blown her off.

For what?

There were women in the medical profession he could imagine being casual and easy to date. Rose Chance was not one of them. Everything about her made him wary.

So why could he not stop thinking about her?

Why could he not stop thinking about that stupid, semi-drunk kiss?

Fourteen

THE DAY OF the wedding dawned. If weather was an omen, Rose thought, as she pulled her blinds and stared out at the new day, then this was a day for an execution, not a wedding. The river was gunmetal grey, the sky heavy and ominous. She felt like it was holding onto the rain until the very moment the bridal party headed for the church. Not unusual weather for this time of year in the Pacific Northwest, but still, she'd hoped.

Theresa was remarkably cool about the bad weather since she'd been watching the forecast all week and all week the grim day had been on the charts with its little square picture of bulky gray clouds spilling raindrops.

"It will be fine. Cozy, even," Theresa said. The venue was a mansion built in the mid 1800s and one of the top wedding spots in the city. All the festivities were indoors but still it would have been nice to gaze out on the eighteen acres of gardens and see them sun-dappled rather than rain-soaked.

The bridal party had gathered at a hotel suite Theresa's parents had rented. They'd driven up from

Hidden Falls the day before and booked it so that the bride and her attendants could leave from the suite together.

Theresa was glowing with happiness, and totally together. Rose imagined she'd be a wreck on her wedding day, knowing this was her last chance to back out, but Theresa obviously had no second thoughts. She was serene under pressure. She'd be a perfect politician's wife. Harvey had chosen well.

The other bridesmaids were also in good shape. All but Kimberly who looked pale, her eyes as wide as a doe's during hunting season.

"Are you all right?" Please let her not be coming down with something that was either catching or that Rose would miss the wedding taking care of.

She blinked. "Sorry. I'm fine. It's such a big day, a wedding."

"I know. But we'll all do great," Rose said, and cupped the side of her neck in affection, which also allowed her to check the woman's pulse and temperature. Temp was normal but her pulse rate was elevated. Rose made a mental note to keep an eye on her.

Then, before she knew it, they were off in two limos. The bouquets, like the dresses, were tasteful and understated. Rose had spent her first couple of hours today at the salon so she knew her hair and makeup were perfect. The dress fit in all the right places, the shoes were comfortable enough. She was excited about having a whole day to enjoy herself.

The wedding itself passed in a blur. This was her third time as a bridesmaid, so she was experienced without feeling jaded. She liked Theresa and Harvey and thought they were good together so it was easy to be part of the sendoff.

As the tallest bridesmaid, she was the last to head up the aisle, right before the bride. When it was her turn, she whispered a last, "Good luck," to Theresa, beaming on the arm of her proud-looking father. She was smiling as she walked up the aisle.

Ahead were the other bridesmaids taking their places. There was Harvey looking as serious as she'd ever seen him. He wasn't the hottest guy in the world, but he had style and plenty of ambition. Beside him were a couple of guys she knew only vaguely, and then her gaze hit on Matt. For a nanosecond she actually didn't recognize him.

In sloppy scrubs, with three-day stubble and a mess of unruly curls, he was pretty hot. In a tux, with his face smooth and his hair recently trimmed, the man was drop dead gorgeous. Or stop dead gorgeous since that's what she did. She missed a step and stood there like a fool, rooted to the spot for the time it took for time to stand still, her eyes to blink, and the world to right itself again.

He was watching her and she felt suddenly breathless. She pasted her smile back on and walked forward once more hoping no one had noticed her stall. Hoping he hadn't noticed.

The ceremony passed as they all do. Vows were recited, hymns sung, no one had any cause why the wedding couldn't take place. Tears were shed, photos were snapped.

Then they were free to mingle until dinner. Matt ended up staying by her side as they headed into the mansion's library where the guests were already enjoying drinks and little nibbly things passed around on trays. "You clean up nicely," she said, feeling that his transformation deserved some comment.

"Thanks. Truth is my mom told me to get a haircut."

She laughed. "You should talk to your mom more often."

"Ouch." He glanced at her sideways. "I'd say you clean up nice too, but I've only ever seen you clean. Be nice to see you dirty some time."

She glanced at him sharply but his gaze was as innocent as a baby's.

"Let me buy you a drink," he said.

"It's a hosted bar. The drinks are free."

"In that case, let me get you a double."

"White wine, please." She scanned the room. "You can bring it to me over there. I'll be with my date."

"Your date?" She had the satisfaction of knowing she'd startled him. Good.

"Yes. My date."

"Should I get him a white wine too?"

"I'm sure he can take care of himself."

She had no idea whether Matt would turn up or not, but she didn't want her brother to be stuck standing alone in a room full of people he didn't know. In a very short time she saw Matt striding her way, a glass of wine in one hand and a beer in the other.

He smiled when he saw her brother, passed her wine and then shook James's hand with his now free one.

"Good to see you, James. Glad you came."

"It's a nice party."

Matt turned to her. "Your brother here was the highlight of the stag. He's not only a great teacher when you get him on the rifle range but he got rid of two drunk assholes who were getting loud and obnoxious so smoothly they never knew what hit them. Seriously, it was poetry in motion."

James shook his head, grinning. "I got them on the bus by letting them think we were all getting on with them. They were so busy arguing they probably drove ten miles before they noticed they were the only two apart from the driver. He got them both home and came back for us. Simple."

"Well, as the guy who organized the stag I can tell you I wouldn't have got rid of them so quietly. So thanks."

"Anytime."

Kimberly walked by. Actually, she looked more like she was creeping, stepping lightly so as not to wake someone up. She was still holding her bridesmaid bouquet and it was shaking. She was still pale. She stood, irresolute and Rose said, "I've got my eye on Kimberly. I think she's coming down with something. She's trembling and very pale. I thought it was nerves but the wedding's over."

"You her doc?" Matt asked, also gazing at the bridesmaid with a professional eye.

"No. Interested bystander."

"She's not sick," James said. He'd followed Rose's gaze and had been watching the young woman too.

"How do you know?"

"She's terrified. You may know illness, but I know fear. Excuse me." And he strode off in the direction of

Kimberly. She hoped, now that he was out of uniform, that he wouldn't terrify the poor woman as he had the first time they'd met. As Rose watched, he joined the small group where she was standing, introduced himself around as though he were simply a wedding guest being friendly. When he got to the supposedly terrified woman, Rose watched the gentleness with which he spoke with her.

"I didn't know your brother was the bridesmaid whisperer," Matt said.

"Neither did I." in fact, there was a lot she didn't know about her brother James. "He's always had a soft spot for anything wounded, though."

"Is he right?"

"I don't know. She didn't have a fever when I checked earlier, but her pulse was elevated. But what's she got to be frightened of at her cousin's wedding?"

"I don't know. But now he's got his eye on her, I can have you all to myself."

Her gaze flew to his. "Do you want me all to yourself?"

He smiled at her in a very disturbing way. "Yes."

Corny lines like that did not make Rose all gooey and fluttery.

Usually.

For some reason, she felt both at his completely honest answer.

When he reached for her hand, she let him lead her out of the crowded library to a quiet alcove that had probably been a pantry or parlor or something back in the mansion's heyday. "Have you heard that bridesmaids always want to get laid or something?"

He appeared shocked. "No. Do they?"

He was ridiculously cute. And they weren't at work and it was a party. She sipped her wine. "I haven't made an exhaustive study, but I have attended a few weddings in my time. This is my third stint as a bridesmaid."

"Third?"

"Mmm. Anyway, I have certainly witnessed some unlikely hook ups which, I think, had a lot to do with alcohol consumption and the air of romance and happily ever after that surrounds a wedding."

"From your tone it sounds like you don't believe in happily ever after."

She was actually startled. "Really?"

"I don't know. Do you?"

She contemplated his words. "I see happy couples. My parents are absurdly happy, as you witnessed." She reflected back on what she'd said. "I think my tone was more critical of people who hook up with bad choices because they get caught up in the romance of the moment." There. That sounded reasonable.

"Okay."

"Are we back at that love at first sight thing you were previously obsessed about?"

He closed his eyes briefly. "I am never going to live that down, am I?"

"Your night of drunken debauchery?"

"It was a stag. Drunken debauchery is not only expected, it's required. It was talking about love at first sight that put me in no man's land."

"You were sort of adorable. And you weren't that drunk."

He moved closer. "Not so drunk that I don't

remember kissing you." He dropped his voice to a low tone that sent a shiver down her spine. "Not so drunk that I don't remember how you tasted."

An eternal moment passed. "What did I taste like?"

Amusement and desire flickered deep in his eyes. "Spearmint."

"Spearmint?" Damn, he really did remember. "I brushed my teeth before I left the house."

He placed a finger over her lips. "I wasn't finished. You tasted like spearmint and something else. Like sex."

"Sex has a flavor?" She meant to sound tough and sassy but her words came out husky and she suspected they could both hear her panties melting right off her.

He took the wine glass out of her hand and set it on a shelf. He set his beer beside it. Then he turned back. His hands went to her waist. If she'd been wearing jeans she thought he'd have hooked his fingers in the belt loops and pulled her closer. His hands felt warm through the fabric of the dress.

"Sex has many flavors. This is one of them," and then he cupped the back of her head and put his mouth over hers. Oh, it was different this time. Stronger, headier. This man wasn't under the influence of scotch. He was in complete control. Of the moment, of her response. He'd lunged at her hungrily in the car after the stag. This time, he teased, wooed. He toyed with her mouth, not dragging a response from her but inviting one.

She'd had a tough time resisting the inebriated Matt. Sober and out to seduce, he was irresistible.

When he pulled back, a quizzical expression on his face, she took over, kissing him back. If he could tease, excite, seduce with nothing but a kiss and whispered promises, so could she.

And she did.

Fifteen

"THERE YOU ARE!" A cheerful voice hailed them. It was Sarah, not only a chatterbox but also one of the biggest gossips in all of Oregon. Fortunately, she'd already pulled away from Matt and was at that moment repairing her lipstick. Sarah's gaze darted from one to the other.

"I hope I'm not interrupting anything?" she said, so clearly hoping otherwise that Rose could see her mentally composing her Facebook post as she stood there.

"Actually, you did interrupt something. Something pretty important," Matt said easily.

If she kicked him Sarah would notice, ditto if she glared at him so she set her teeth and waited, wondering how much damage control would be required after he'd puffed out his chest and pounded on it for a while.

"Rose was asking my advice about one of her patients who has a heart condition. You know how it is, when you have superior knowledge, it's good to share."

Her jaw dropped. As a way to deflect the nosy bridesmaid's attention from any idea that they'd been passionately kissing mere seconds ago, suggesting they were discussing a patient was a brilliant ruse. But to paint her as needing his superior advice? She almost thought she'd rather have Sarah broadcasting their clandestine make-out session.

"Whatever," Sarah replied, obviously uninterested in any conversation that lacked gossip value. "It's almost time for dinner and speeches. Theresa told me to tell you."

"Great. Thanks for coming to find us."

The three of them headed to the ballroom together, but Sarah headed off to the washroom. As soon as she was out of sight, Rose smacked Matt lightly on the arm. "Your superior knowledge? Seriously?"

He looked like he was thoroughly enjoying himself and completely unrepentant. "What? I had to say something. I could tell her about this sound you make when you start getting turned on. It's not a purr, or a growl exactly, kind of a–"

"Thank you. I get it." She would not blush. She was a medical professional, a woman of thirty-one. So what if she had been mixing it up with one very sexy surgeon. They were both single. Why shouldn't they?

A thought hit her like a bucket of ice water dumped over her head. Theresa had said his love life was in the 'it's complicated' territory.

She turned to him, amid the noisy chaos of two hundred guests finding their places in the big banquet hall. "Wait a minute. You are single aren't you?"

"What kind of a question is that? Of course I'm single."

"Okay, good." But she scanned his face.

"You said that like you think I'm lying."

"No. It's just that Theresa said your relationship status was 'it's complicated.'"

He looked smug rather than guilty. "You asked about me?"

"No!" And how stupid to give him any reason to think she had. "Someone else asked. I overheard."

He put a hand under her elbow and shepherded her toward the top table where they were both seated. "I did have a mostly casual relationship. But that's over now."

"Oh. When did it end?"

He winced like this was not a question he'd been prepared for. "Wednesday."

She glanced at him. "Wednesday, as in three days ago?"

"Yes. That Wednesday."

She allowed herself a moment to feel flattered. Of course, he and his casual friend could have broken up for all kinds of reasons, but she thought the timing was significant. Wednesday was the day he'd come to apologize for kissing her the night of the stag. Wednesday was the day he'd told her that this was not over. She didn't say any more, simply filed that nugget of information away.

The wedding banquet was both the same as every other wedding banquet she'd ever attended and different. There were the speeches, the predictable banquet food, the first dance, the hugs, the tears. When it was time for Theresa to throw her bouquet, Rose only took part because she'd look conspicuous if she didn't. However, she made certain to stand far back. She had no plans to marry anytime soon and no interest in some ridiculous tradition that involved fighting other women for second-hand flowers.

Theresa, however, had been a jock in school and still worked out regularly. When she threw her bouquet over her head she put everything she had into her throw so the large bouquet exploded into the air as though from a rocket-launcher, sailed up and over her head and blasted into the heavy crystal chandelier.

The bouquet had lasted through hours of being carried, set down, picked up again, and dropped a time or two. The chandelier had hung, gracious and elegant for the better part of two centuries. The impact of bouquet with chandelier was more than either was built to withstand. As the huge bouquet hit the enormous light fixture, sparkles of light, blooms and rose petals exploded into the air. Showers of lily, rose, green fern, some yellow scented thing, and bits of wire and ribbon rained down. Rose felt a confetti of plant material hit her head and shoulders and one perfect, white rosebud sailed in front of her so she instinctively reached for it before it fell to the floor.

Amid the laughter and exclamations, she retreated back to her seat, brushing fern from her shoulders.

Matt, of course, had witnessed the entire thing. He was laughing as he came over and sat with her. "Theresa should seriously think about competing in the Highland Games. She'd be a serious contender at tossing the caber."

She chuckled, and said, "Is there florist's wire in my hair?"

He reached up and picked off a yellow petal. "Now you're flawless again."

"Good."

He gestured to the white bud in her hand. "What does it mean, exactly, if you catch a rosebud?"

They both contemplated the unfurled blossom. "I guess it means I'll marry someone very small."

"With very tiny . . . thorns."

Theresa came by soon after. "Listen guys, heads up," she yelled to the bridal party still at the table. "We're not going to run off like the etiquette books say we're supposed to. We both love to party and these are all our favorite people. Harv and I plan to close this party down. So that means you guys can leave whenever. You don't have to be polite and wait for us to leave."

"Good to know. Thanks."

Matt turned to her. "Would you like to dance?"

She felt mild surprise. "You dance?"

"Mostly I stand there and jiggle."

She smiled and nodded. And, naturally, Matt turned out to be an excellent dancer. As they stepped onto the wooden floor the music changed to a slow dance and he pulled her to him. She felt herself move in harmony with the man, enjoying his warm, athletic body. When the dance ended he said, "Let's get out of here."

"But, my date. James is planning to drive me home."

"I think James might have other plans."

As she followed his gaze she saw her brother with the waiflike bridesmaid, who was starting to get some color back. When he saw her looking his way he gestured subtly for her to come over.

She did and he said, "I think Kimberly's tired. I'm

driving her home."

She looked Kimberly over rapidly. She no longer looked quite so sick and the trembling had stopped. "Okay."

"Can you get a ride?" He didn't by so much as the flicker of an eyelid indicate Matt standing beside her.

"Sure. I can find my own way home."

She smiled at the waif. "It was really nice being in the wedding party with you."

"You too."

After they left, Matt turned to her. "So? Can I drive you home?"

She glanced around and found that about half the guests were gone. Theresa and Harvey were twirling on the dance floor. No one would even notice if they slipped away. "Sure."

"Great."

She gathered up her purse and headed for the cloakroom. Matt followed. When he helped her put on her coat she noticed he was holding the rosebud that had all but fallen on her from Theresa's bouquet. "Why did you bring the flower?"

"I thought you would want to press it, keep it in a scrapbook and dream of the man you would one day marry."

"You've been watching too many movies on the Lifetime Channel."

"Sad to see it die."

She shook her head and they headed out into the cold night across the parking lot toward his small 4×4 truck. He opened her door and held it for her.

Getting into the thing involved hiking up her skirt.

And climbing. "Why do you have a truck?"

"Comes in handy for hauling things. Also, I do a lot of backcountry skiing and hiking. The 4X4 gets me places nothing else will."

At least the interior was clean.

They didn't talk much on the way to her place. She directed him and when they arrived she felt a jump of nerves. The entire evening had been heading in a certain direction, but did she really want to go there?

She glanced over at him. He looked gorgeous, a little mysterious, and she thought how very tired she was of her own rules and of being so careful all the time. So, this would probably end up messy, neither of them had time to devote to anything long term. It would be a hook-up, probably. Was she okay with that?

She watched his capable surgeon's hands on the wheel and her body ached for him.

Yes, she was okay with that.

When he pulled into one of the guest parking spots behind her building, leaving the engine idling, she turned to him. "Do you want to come up?"

"About as much as I want the blood to keep pumping around my body."

She smiled. "Are you going to tell anyone?"

He seemed to consider her question. "Probably only Sarah. She should take care of making sure every person at the wedding knows we went home together. And I'm a personal friend of Fred Armisen. I'm sure I could get him to do an episode of *Portlandia* about us." His eyes twinkled as he teased her.

As if. She nodded briskly. "Okay, then. Come on." She pushed open her door and jumped down. He turned off the truck engine and followed her. She almost dropped her key fob in her haste. Now that she'd decided she was going to sleep with mouthwatering Matt she felt jumpy.

She never got involved with people she worked with for good reason. What if he fell in love with her or turned out to be a crazy stalker or something?

Stop it! She headed for the elevator, feeling him behind her as hot as his kisses earlier. Inside the elevator he pulled her to him as though he couldn't wait. He was less subtle than he'd been at the wedding, more like a man who has definite plans and a very good idea how to accomplish them.

She smiled to herself. She liked a man who knew what he was doing around a woman's body. One of her greatest shocks in medical school had been discovering how many doctors had no clue.

They walked in and she flipped on a light. Matt came behind her and eased off her coat, kissed the back of her neck, sending shivers of desire rippling down her skin.

"Would you like some wine?"

"I would," he said.

"Come in and make yourself comfortable."

He walked into her main room and toured around, touching things. He was a very tactile person, she'd noticed it before. He was a toucher.

"Nice place," he said.

"Thanks."

"This is an interesting piece." The pottery vase was blue and shaped like a woman's torso, but slightly off, so you had to look twice. Rose wasn't entirely sure the look was intentional. "Thanks. My mother made it."

He ran his fingertips over the curving lines of the piece in a way that made her imagine the feel of those hands on her own skin. "Your mother's an artist?"

"Oh, she'd love to hear you say that. Mostly she thinks of herself as a potter. Her works can be hit or miss, but I love that one."

She walked into the kitchen and opened her wine fridge, grabbed the first bottle her hand touched, and turned to find Matt right behind her. He held up the rose. "We should put this in water."

"Right." She put the wine down on the granite countertop and opened the glass-fronted cupboard where she kept wineglasses. On the top shelf sat a glass bud vase. When she would have reached for it, he said, "I got it," and took the vase down. He ran some water and then plopped the single rosebud into the vase.

Then he reached over, cupped her head and pulled her toward him, kissing her deeply.

When they came up for air, she said, "The wine?"

"I'm not that thirsty." He kissed her again and she felt her blood start to heat. "What I'd really like is to see the rest of your apartment."

"Okay."

She pulled back, took his hand and walked him back through the living room, down a short hall. "I don't believe you've seen my bedroom."

She flipped on the chandelier as she entered. While the rest of her apartment was sleek and modern, her bedroom was her private retreat. She'd worked with a designer and gone with a completely feminine room since she had no one to please but herself. Through her lust haze she imagined how her room looked through Matt's eyes. The chandelier sparkled like something out of a fairy tale, casting soft light on the purple and silver bedspread. The soft gray walls were framed with white trim.

Since she liked to sit in bed and watch TV on the odd lazy evening at home, she had a heap of pillows on the bed. She kept the TV behind the doors of a white cabinet. Her artwork was a combination of an original sea scene she'd bought on holiday, and a couple of nudes she'd seen at a gallery opening for an up-and-coming artist.

"Nice," he said, going to stand before one of the nudes, running a finger across the bottom of the frame. She felt as though he were running that fingertip across her skin. "I'd like to see you in that pose. With that look on your face."

She crossed the hardwood floor to her bedside, flipping on one of the crystal lamps she'd purchased at an antique store. The soft light illuminated the designer bedside tables and the headboard.

Matt flipped off the overhead switch so the room became immediately more dimly lit.

For a moment she felt the grip of uncertainty. What had she done? Or, more to the point, what was she contemplating doing? Whatever happened tonight, they would still cross paths professionally. There were reasons she never dated anyone in the medical profession. Not that this was dating, of course. She didn't know what it was.

As she turned to him, wondering if she should call the evening over, she found him already in front of her.

The man moved like a panther.

He pulled her against him, so she bumped chest to chest, feeling his strength once more. All it took was one touch and she gave up thinking. He had enough sureness for both of them.

He tipped back her head, taking full advantage of her mouth, kissing her as though all he'd ever wanted in the entirety of his life was to kiss her lips, push his hands through the heavy weight of her hair. She was moving way too fast from zero to *oh, yes, yes, YES!!* She could hear her pulse pounding as he moved his mouth on hers, teasing her with his tongue. She could taste beer and hot, healthy male.

Too much clothing was between them. She helped him slip off his jacket and, slob that he was, he let it slide to the floor in a black heap. She threw her arms around him and rubbed her hands down his back enjoying the feel of his strong muscles enticing her beneath his shirt.

Before she could plunge her hands beneath the cotton to the hot skin, he eased the zipper of her bridesmaid dress slowly down her back. Her skin was so sensitive she felt the slide, the parting of fabric like a caress.

He kissed her again, and, with his clever surgeon's hands, had her dress sliding off her shoulders before she noticed he was undressing her. As the navy fabric slid to pool in darkness at her feet, he held her away from him, his gaze devouring her breasts in the brand new lingerie she was so glad she'd worn. It had been a genius idea to have the hen party in a lingerie store. The gift certificate had been enough for Theresa to buy a stunning silk and lace nightgown for her wedding night, plus a few fun items to tease Harvey with on their honeymoon.

The woman who owned the store had offered all of them a twenty percent discount on anything they bought that night and as she'd poured them all wine, they'd bonded over corsets and camisoles, stockings and silks. As Rose had dithered between a sinful black creation that showcased her breasts and a much more practical bra and panties set, Theresa had said, "You know, women often decide whether they are going to have sex with a man when they pick out their underwear. I mean, before they go out."

"What are you? A sex anthropologist?" Sarah had scoffed.

"No. A magazine junkie. If I'm not reading Modern Bride I'm reading those women's magazines, you know the ones that tell you Top Ten Ways to Make Him Yell out Your Name in Bed. Complete with quizzes. The point is, if you wear sexy underwear you're more likely to get laid."

Even as she'd scoffed at Theresa's magazine research, Rose had chosen the black set, all lace and silk and hot fantasy.

Now that Matt was looking at her as though he'd lost the ability to form words, she was happy she'd listened to Theresa. And the bride had been right. There was something about slipping into decadent lingerie that definitely put a girl in the mood.

It seemed to be working on Matt, too.

"You," he kissed the top of one breast, "Are," he kissed the top of the other, "Sensational."

Then he pulled her against him, crushing her lips

with his mouth, his hands going everywhere at once. His greed and impatience fired hers. She dragged at his shirt, wished he was wearing his usual sloppy scrubs rather than making her deal with the intricacies of a tux.

She almost growled in frustration as she fumbled with shirt studs until he pushed her hands away and did the job himself, though not very smoothly. He shoved the black dress slacks down his legs, kicking them off with impatience.

His skin had the permanent suntan darkness of his Greek blood, and he was hairy in all the places she liked a man to be hairy.

Pushing back the coverlet on the bed, he gently pushed her so she fell into the soft, luxurious sheets.

As she gazed her fill at that glorious man standing beside the bed, he bent and slipped out of his plaid boxers. Then he stared down at her.

"Who'd have thought," he said, his voice a husky whisper, "that you owned underwear like that."

"You like it?"

He reached out and stroked her chest, over her lace-covered nipple, and down to her belly. "I like what's in it," he said.

So the right answer.

Sixteen

HE FOLLOWED HER down onto the bed, his body hot and needy against hers. His hands were everywhere, exciting her, learning her. Her skin was pale against his darkness, soft against his hardness. And yet his mouth was so soft, tender almost as it traced the line of her collarbone, dipping to her breasts. He studied the corset bra for a moment as though it were a puzzle. Then he reached and slipped the black silk bow open.

She sighed as he leaned forward and licked the skin he'd exposed.

Unhooking each of the front hooks was as complicated as the studs on his dress shirt, but he took his time, opening each one as though it were a gift. The sensations were racing too fast for her to keep up. Her nipples ached for his touch.

And as he put his mouth on one sensitive point, he reached down, slipping his hand into her panties, sliding to her core where she was already slick with desire and playing with her even as his mouth was busy at her breast.

Orgasm one hit her so fast she barely had time to register how close she was. She arched against his fingers, pushing herself against him. He took her lead, giving her what she needed until her back arched right off the bed and her cries echoed off the walls.

He stroked her softly, bringing her down slowly, kissing her easily until her sobbing breath subsided.

"That was—not supposed to happen so fast. It's, um, been a while."

His smile was cat-got-the-cream satisfied. "Amazing," he said. "That was absolutely amazing."

His arousal was throbbing against her thigh. She said, "Condoms are in the side table."

"Not so fast," he said, rising so he could look down at her probably flushed face. "Can you do that again?"

A warm flood of possibilities filled her. She tilted her head, glanced up through her lashes. "Let's find out."

"Oh, I do like a challenge."

"I want you inside me."

"Strangely, I want that too." He might joke, but she felt the quiver in his skin. He was controlling himself with an effort. He reached for her night table, and she watched him sheath himself, swiftly and efficiently.

And as he slowly entered her body she felt stretched in places she didn't think she'd ever been stretched. "Oh," she moaned, "Oh."

"You okay?" He stopped, holding her still.

She turned her head until she could kiss him. "I am so much more than okay," she whispered.

He moved slowly at first, and then faster until she felt the shockwaves begin to rise until she quaked and cried out and stars exploded behind her eyelids.

Matt stayed with her and right when she thought she couldn't take any more she felt him shudder and burst into a language that had to be Greek.

When their breath had returned to something approaching normal, she said, "What did you yell out at the end there?"

"I yelled?" he blinked at her from sexy hazel eyes.

"You did. In Greek, I think. Was it my name?"

She felt him shrug. "Might have been."

She thought of Theresa and her magazine articles and felt her own cat-got-the-cream smugness. "Good."

Then she turned her head. "That was a lot of condoms you put on the table."

His teeth flashed white as he grinned. "Waste not, want not."

* * *

ROSE WOKE SUDDENLY, wondering why she was so hot, and then became aware that a very warm male body was pressed up against hers. In that instant of rising from sleep to full consciousness, memories flooded back. They'd never discussed Matt staying the night; she suspected they'd both dropped into exhausted sleep at some point.

Dawn was letting a gauzy film of light into the room, enough for her to watch him sleeping and admire the strong features that made up his face. She was reminded of the Greek statues she'd admired when she traveled through Europe. His nose was strong, his jaw determined, his lips full and soft in sleep.

She ran her fingertip along the line of his jaw, rough with stubble. He stirred and mumbled something but was soon deeply asleep once more.

She rolled out of bed and headed for the kitchen where she started coffee. Then she followed her usual Sunday morning routine. She crept past him into her ensuite bathroom and showered, then grabbed clean clothes and dressed in the guest bedroom, which she mostly used as a home office.

She was in the kitchen enjoying her first cup of coffee and checking the news on her tablet when he walked in looking heavy-eyed and scrumptious. Naturally, he didn't have any clothes with him so he'd pulled on his boxer shorts and wore her bathrobe over top.

He should have looked ridiculous.

He looked mouthwateringly delicious. "Coffee?"

"Thanks."

She didn't feel like asking how he liked his coffee, as though she were his waitress, so she poured him a mug and pushed the sugar pot toward him. "Milk's in the fridge."

He nodded, yawned and picked up the mug, drinking the coffee black.

She wished she still took a real newspaper so she could pass him a section, but she didn't. No way to share news that arrived digitally.

He didn't seem too bothered. He picked up his coffee and headed to the living room where he stood staring out at the view.

No way to tell what he was thinking from his profile. He remained silent. Finally, she said, "Should we talk about this?"

"Talk about what?"

She put down her coffee mug with a snap. "Why do men do that? *Talk about what?* I'm not interested in discussing local politics, the weather or religion. So take a wild guess."

A flash of humor lit his face. "Sex. You want to talk about sex."

"Well, not exactly what I was getting at but you're on the right track."

He stepped closer. "The sex was great."

"It was." Great didn't even begin to describe it. Even though they'd barely slept she felt full of energy, her body still thrumming. "I mean–" She had no idea how to phrase what she was trying to say. She wished she'd kept her mouth shut. But she hadn't, and he was looking at her as though she was going to propose or something, so she snapped, "I mean, is this a one time thing?" No, that wasn't it either. Why could she not think clearly?

He sipped coffee, regarding her over the rim of the mug. "Do you want it to be a one time thing?"

"Quit turning everything back on me. What do *you* want?"

"I want to have a shower and get my head together. I want to take you out for breakfast. But not in my tux. That's what I want."

"Kind of short-term thinking."

"All I'm capable of right now."

"Sorry, I'm being Type A about this. We don't work together exactly but obviously our worlds are connected. I don't want any awkwardness. I think we should be clear about boundaries."

"Boundaries?" He looked at her as though she were speaking a language he was unfamiliar with.

"You know, figuring out how and when we can see each other and making absolutely certain to be discreet about this."

"Why does it matter so much to you that no one know anything about this?"

"Because the hospital is a hot bed of gossip. I do not care to be the subject of gossip."

"Hate to be the one to break it to you, but you already are."

Shock had her eyes opening wide. "What?"

He shrugged. "People talk about how you walk down a hospital corridor like it's a runway. You overdress. Stuff like that."

Even though it irked her that hospital staff had nothing better to do than criticize her fashion choices, he was making her point for her. "If they go after my high heels can you imagine the field day they'd have about my sex life?"

"Why do you care so much? We're both single. It's not like we're hurting anyone."

She was starting to feel hot and claustrophobic. "I keep my private life private."

"Okay. So, how do you see this working?"

She shook her head. "I never date doctors. It's too complicated, with schedules and lack of time."

"Rose, we both get time off. Why don't we spend a bit of it with each other and see what happens?" He didn't add *like normal people,* but the words hovered behind his words like a silent addition to the sentence.

He smiled in a most disturbing way, getting her body humming again. "Like today, for instance. I'm off work, you're off work. We could do something."

"I have plans today. I need to catch up on paperwork. Do my laundry." Damn, she wished she hadn't mentioned the laundry. It wasn't that laundry was more important than Matt. But she needed to be absolutely clear about boundaries.

He seemed puzzled by her response. "Okay. You do your laundry. Get caught up on your paperwork. How about dinner? Can I take you for dinner tonight?"

"I don't know. I have to think about it."

"Okay." He gulped more coffee then headed back to her bedroom. He emerged a minute later with his tux thrown on and not done up properly.

"How's your dad?"

Rose regarded him. "Are you asking as his doctor?"

His eyes narrowed slightly as though he wasn't certain how to answer. "No. I guess not. I think I'm asking mostly because it's your dad. Is that a problem?"

Was it a problem? Her body still hummed from their night together and now he was asking about members of her family, so she got the feeling that he might have misunderstood whatever this thing was between them. Although, how could you misunderstand something that had no definition? No substance? She felt that it was up to her to provide some ground rules. Guidance for both of them. That sounded mature, sensible, like a woman in control of her body and her life.

"I like you, Matt, I do. Last night was great. But let's not make it more than it was."

He stepped towards her, his eyes going flat. "Okay.

So, I don't get to ask about your dad? Even though I operated on him?"

He didn't remind her of the way she'd run after him, practically charged into the shower stall, and all but begged him to take her father's emergency case. She sighed. "I'm being a complete bitch. I'm sorry." How to explain her feelings when she didn't understand them herself? "I don't like moving too fast. You're already in my life, now you're in my brother's life and my dad's life too."

He didn't call her on the fact that she was the one who had brought him into both her brother's life and her dad's, and it was hard not to appreciate that.

He set down his coffee mug. "I like your brother. He's a good guy."

"I know. He liked you, too." She was sure that when she wasn't so tired she would be able to think more clearly. "And, my dad is doing well. Not bouncing back, but I keep telling him it takes time."

Matt nodded. "It's denial."

"What is?"

"It's sort of a guy thing. I see it a lot. Men get to a certain age, and they don't want to admit that they're slowing down, things maybe aren't working the way they used to, then they have a crisis. They suffer a heart attack, fall off the roof when they're putting up their Christmas lights, they have a stroke, and suddenly they're faced with the fact that they're getting older. And so, instead of slowing down they do the opposite. They push themselves harder, tell themselves whatever happened was a fluke, and generally put their families through hell.

She was nodding before he got halfway through his explanation. She'd seen it in her own practice, but she'd never imagined her dad, laidback Jack Chance, would be one of those stubborn men. She supposed she hadn't been able to see the obvious because she was too close. "You're right. Of course. I'll have a talk with him. Maybe I can get him to slow down a little."

"And somebody will have to make sure he gets himself a regular GP. He needs to be monitored."

She knew that. Did he think she didn't know that? Who's father was this? Finally, she turned to him. "Look, you're a great guy. A really great guy. But I don't do this."

He looked confused. "Don't do what exactly?"

She threw her arms around like a demented windmill. "This. I don't do this. Relationships with people I work with. Especially not with doctors."

Instead of backing off gracefully, he stared at her. "Why not?"

"Because it's too complicated. Too claustrophobic. Too sticky. I thought you felt the same way."

"Not really. Especially not the sticky part. Makes me sound like fly paper."

They stood there awkwardly for a moment. How to say goodbye? After a bout of sex so incredible it was starting to feel like a fantasy, was she going to kiss him on the cheek? Pat him on the back?

He took the decision away from her, leaning in and kissing her swiftly on the lips. As he pulled away she was aware of a sudden and crazy urge to cling, to wrap her arms around him and pull him closer.

But before the crazy idea had made it from her brain

to her lips, he was looking for his truck keys.

"Thanks for a great night," he said, "I'll call you."

And he was gone.

She wandered slowly back into her kitchen feeling suddenly like she'd been rude. She could have offered him breakfast. But he'd get the wrong idea. She had to be careful with this one.

The white rose sat on the counter where they'd left it last night, along with the wine bottle she'd taken out of her wine fridge.

She returned the wine to the fridge. Then she moved the rosebud to her coffee table. The tightly furled bud was already beginning to open.

Seventeen

OF COURSE, AFTER she'd explained to Matt all about her boundaries, she couldn't seem to impose them on herself.

She thought about him all day.

She thought about him when she was doing paperwork, and when she changed her sheets and did the laundry. When she found a lone, black, man's sock under the bed, she sat down and slipped the sock over her hand, and then had an animated conversation with the sock puppet. Basically practicing what she'd say when he called.

But he didn't call.

When she reviewed the way she'd treated him this morning, which she could see was a lot more related to her own panic than his behavior, she had to accept that she'd been a twit. Unfortunately, the sock puppet agreed.

Finally, she called him.

He answered right away, which she thought was a good sign.

He was panting, which could mean anything.

"Catch you at a bad time?"

"Gym," he said.

"Oh, sorry."

"No problem. What's up?"

Her libido, but she didn't admit that, obviously. She said, "I have something of yours."

"Really?" his voice turned from terse to much warmer. "Is it something important?"

A single black sock for a guy who mostly wore gym socks or bare feet? She gazed at the black sock folded neatly on her couch. "Vital."

"Well, I'd better swing by and pick it up then. Is tonight good for you?"

"Very."

"Say nine or so?"

"See you then."

He didn't mention dinner and she was glad he'd got her message.

When he arrived a few minutes before nine, she was ready. Showered, wearing some of her favorite silky body lotion beneath even silkier lingerie, and with fresh sheets on the bed.

He walked in and she could almost feel his arousal shimmering around him. "Hi," she said.

He kissed her. "Hi."

"Would you like some wine? Or I also have beer."

She thought a hint of emotion, maybe sadness, crossed his face, but that didn't make any sense. She was offering him alcohol and sex. If she threw in a bag of chips she'd be the perfect woman.

"Sure," he said. "A beer would be great."

She poured him his beer, knowing that if she left it

to him he'd drink from the bottle, and poured herself a glass of wine.

When she returned, he was holding up the sock with a question in his eyes.

"I knew how much you'd need it. All those black tie events you attend."

"And me owning only one pair of black socks," he agreed, and then he took the drinks out of her hands and kissed her, more hungrily this time.

"I thought about you all day," he told her in a husky tone.

"I don't date other medical professionals," she explained, running her hand over his jaw and discovering he'd shaved.

"No. Of course not. It's a terrible idea."

"Surgeons are arrogant."

"The worst," he agreed, running his lips over her shoulder. How had she never noticed that her shoulder was one of her most sensitive erogenous zones? Her shoulder?

She pulled at his gray T-shirt and he helped her strip it off. His skin was warm, and whatever time he was putting in at the gym was paying off.

"And most GPs think they're God."

She pulled back slightly. "Most GPs?"

"Some GPs," he amended. There was a stretch between her shoulder and the top of her breast that, of course, she knew as the pectoral muscle, but when his lips traced a course down the slope she discovered yet another one of her previously unacknowledged hot zones.

"So, we won't date," she said, determined to hang

onto her sense long enough to finish this conversation.

"Terrible idea," he murmured. She wasn't entirely sure he was listening to her every word. His mouth had now reached the top of her breast and while every fool knew the breast was a highly erogenous area of the body, hers seemed to have grown even more receptive in the last couple of minutes.

Her head tipped back giving him greater access, but she felt the brush of his dark curls against her chin. "So, we won't."

"We definitely won't."

Then he began to ease her out of her robe and she was lost.

Later they lay together, too lazy and sated to move, his hand lying on her breast as though he'd forgotten it was there. She liked the warm feel of his skin against hers more than she wanted to like it.

She turned so she was on her side facing him which made his hand fall off of her. "You've done this before, right?"

His sleepy eyes twinkled with humor. "Did I seem like a rank amateur?"

She smacked his shoulder lightly. "Not sex." That he pretty much had his PhD in. "I mean this kind of relationship."

The twinkle faded. "Define 'this kind of relationship.'"

"You know. Casual. Convenient. We're together when it works into our schedules but not committed in any way."

"You mean we're on call?"

"Not how I'd have phrased it, but yes. I got the

feeling that your last relationship was pretty casual."

"Absolutely, it was."

"So, you don't have a problem with casual?"

"You worried I'll start serenading you under your windows at night and follow you around like a lost dog?"

She shuddered. He wouldn't be the first. Okay, she'd only been serenaded that once, and the midnight crooner had been both drunk and Italian, which pretty much gave him a pass on over-the-top romantic gestures, but she hadn't been able to face returning to Venice since the unfortunate incident. "Definitely no serenading."

"I think I've got it." He flopped onto his back, crossed his hands over his stomach. Great stomach. Muscular with the light tan that she now knew was a permanent part of his Greek heritage.

He sounded distant, as though she might have offended him in some way, but she knew he was as busy as she was. If they could shoehorn some private time into their busy lives they could enjoy each other without the wasted time of dating, getting to know each other's friends and families, all that time that neither of them had to spare. Of course, he already knew half her family, but there was no way she was telling anyone with the last name Chance that she was getting naked with Dr. Vasilopolous.

Her parents might be old hippies but they had a strangely conservative streak when it came to marriage. One hint that she and Matt were intimate and her mom would be planning the wedding complete with homemade wedding cake and flowers from the garden.

No doubt they'd expect her to dance in the grass barefoot with a daisy chain woven through her hair.

Okay, there'd already been one Chance wedding and it hadn't been like that at all. In fact, Evan and Caitlyn's wedding had been pretty much perfect, even though the festivities *had* taken place in the Chance family garden.

"Good. And can I ask you not to mention anything to James? I know you guys hang out, but I'd appreciate us keeping this . . . whatever it is, to ourselves."

"Complete secrecy. Got it."

He turned his head and she was shocked at how wintry his gaze seemed suddenly. "And are we open to other . . . offers?"

She felt confused. "Open to other offers?" What was this, a real estate transaction?

"Other people."

"Oh." She paused. Thinking. And not liking the cold stone that lodged in the pit of her stomach at the thought of Matt sleeping with anyone else. "I'd prefer to be exclusive." Her throat felt suddenly dry so she swallowed. "Purely for health reasons."

"Okay." He sounded like it didn't much matter either way.

She felt they'd taken a wrong turn somehow and she didn't know exactly how it had happened. It was practical to be clear about the ground rules of this relationship. Since she imagined Matt would be extremely relieved to discover she was no more interested in a messy relationship with any kind of implied commitment than he was, she didn't understand why the mood between them had changed.

"I'm guessing your last relationship was similar?"

His eyes closed briefly and then opened again. "It was exactly like that."

"Tell me about her, the last woman you were, um, involved with."

He looked at her as though she might have been in the sun too long even though they were inside her apartment. "What do you want to know?"

"I don't know. I want to put you in some kind of context, I guess."

"She and I were exactly what you want you and me to be. No strings. Not a lot in common. I was not required to commit to boring events I had no interest in with people I didn't know. I didn't give her a hard time when she went away, and she traveled a lot on business. She didn't bust my balls for working long hours. We liked each other, the sex was good. That's it."

She nodded. Yep, this was exactly the relationship she was proposing to him. And one day she imagined he'd describe her in similar terms. Like a cellphone plan you'd once had that was convenient and didn't drop too many calls, but when a better plan came along with a different provider, he wasn't bound by any loyalty. He'd move on.

"Have you ever been in love?" she asked him.

There was a pause so long she thought he wouldn't answer. "Yeah," he said at last. "Once."

He sounded so sad, she asked, "What happened?"

He turned to her. "Aren't you breaking your own rules here? That's the kind of stuff people talk about when they care about each other."

"Well, I do. I mean, I don't not care."

"How about you? You ever been in love?"

Okay, she'd started this topic. She'd been the one insane enough to bring love into a conversation that was all about casual. What was wrong with her? "I thought I was. Peter Buckingham. I met him in San Francisco at a fundraiser. Some branch of his family had immigrated and brought over a priceless collection of paintings, they built a mansion specifically designed around the art. The place was getting kind of derelict and too expensive for the last of the American Buckinghams to keep up, so, when she died, she left the home and the collection to the people of San Francisco. Which was very generous, except that you need a lot of money to get a derelict mansion back in shape, plus, obviously, there was a lot of security and so on to worry about. Anyway, there was a big fundraising campaign and Peter came over, representing the family, to help raise money. He gave a lot of lectures, appeared at countless fundraisers, even sold himself at a bachelor auction." She grinned in memory. "He was 'bought' by three older ladies who took him to tea and asked him about the queen. I met him pretty early on, and for the next two years, I saw him whenever he was in the states."

"This is the Buckingham Collection you're talking about."

"Yes."

"I've seen it. I've never seen so many Rembrandts in one place." He shifted, so he was on one elbow looking down at her. "Wasn't there some story where he auctioned one of the paintings off to get the money for the repairs?"

"Yes. And it was bought by a rich philanthropist

who then donated it back to the collection, with a discreet plaque of course, crediting them with the donation."

"Yeah, I remember that. Wow, and you dated that guy. Isn't he a prince or something?"

"A baronet. I even flew to London to meet his family. But, I don't know, when he went back to England for good, the relationship kind of fizzled out. It's a long way to go for a weekend."

"Or you didn't want it enough."

"Maybe we didn't love each other enough to try."

It was a wound that had never completely healed. Peter was everything she'd ever dreamed of.

When she'd walked into the family estate she'd felt as though she were walking into *Downton Abbey*. For a few moments she'd been that little girl, that Cinderella who finally gets plucked out from behind the stove and transported magically into a fairy world of Prince Charmings and ball gowns. She'd taken to the life immediately. Would she have married Peter if he'd asked her? Would she have given up the life she'd built here in Portland to move to England and become Lady Buckingham?

Since he hadn't asked her, she'd never know. "And you? Your turn."

"For someone who's into casual, you ask a lot of nosy questions."

"I'm sorry. Have you noticed that I'm a woman?"

"Oh, yeah. I noticed."

She smacked him.

"There's not much to tell. First time I saw her I think I was a goner."

From the tone in his voice it didn't sound like his love was reciprocated. "And she?"

He shook his head. "Not so much. My mother thinks I'm a great catch if I stick to a nice Greek girl she knows from church. My father thinks I can't be too picky."

She chuckled. "I hope you get the woman you want."

"Me too. But in the meantime . . ." he leaned over and tucked her hair out of the way, then kissed her, moving his body against hers so it was pretty clear the conversation was over and he had other things on his mind than talking.

Eighteen

IT WAS AMAZING how quickly they fell into a routine. He'd text her if he had some time, she'd text him if she wanted company. He gave her a copy of his schedule so she knew when he was available. She worked around his basketball nights and he finished a shift exactly as she was heading home from book club.

He stuck to the rules she'd set down perfectly. He didn't invite her out for dinner or movies or to anything involving his friends. Their conversation was almost always about work or something interesting one or the other had seen or done. After that one conversation about love, they stayed off personal topics.

He never spent the night and he never invited her to his place. The only entire night they'd spent together had been the night of Theresa and Harvey's wedding. It was fine, of course. Practical. But she'd never said he couldn't spend the night. They never talked about it. Turned out there was a lot they didn't talk about.

She was surprised when James mentioned he'd taken Matt shooting again and Matt had invited him to join the Wednesday night basketball game any time he was available or in the neighborhood.

The next Wednesday, Matt texted her after basketball:

Hot and sweaty. You interested?

She smiled, feeling her girl parts start to hum in anticipation.

I'll start the shower

When he arrived, he kissed her and she kind of liked the salty sweat taste and the heat coming off his skin. Still, she handed him a blue fluffy towel and pointed him to the bathroom. "I bought you a present," she said, "It's in the bathroom."

He sent her a quizzical look and then headed to the bathroom as directed. "You got me a razor?" He shouted through the closed door.

"Yep."

"Is that a hint?"

"Yep."

"It's pink."

She grinned at the door. "I know. Congratulations, you helped support a cure for breast cancer. And the guy at the drug store said it shaves really close."

"If I was shaving my legs."

She heard the water blast on and went to turn the bed sheets down in her bedroom and set the lighting to exactly the way she liked it. Bright enough to see what they were doing but dim enough to disguise any hint of cellulite that her periodic jogging spells hadn't erased.

He was always fast in the shower. This time he probably took a couple of extra minutes and sure enough, when he entered her bedroom wearing nothing but a towel, she saw how smooth his face looked and figured the guy in the drug store hadn't led her astray.

He stalked forward menacingly, tossed the towel and grabbed her, rubbing his freshly-shaven cheek against her neck. "This smooth enough for you?"

"Yes."

He picked her up and tossed her on the bed, so she shrieked in surprise.

"Are you sure it's soft enough?" he asked. Then he pulled her silky robe off and rubbed his cheek against her belly.

He'd found a ticklish spot so she giggled and squirmed. "Yes."

"Are you absolutely sure?" He rubbed his freshly-shaven face against her breast.

"Yes," she sighed.

Afterward, she said, "Was James at basketball?"

"No. Why?"

"No reason. He mentioned you and he have been shooting and you invited him to your game. I was surprised you never said anything."

"Hey, I'm playing by your rules here."

He was technically correct, but something about him hanging out with her brother and not telling her seemed wrong. "But, he's my brother."

"Well, I don't tell him I'm seeing you, either. It's easier that way."

"I guess."

Somehow, she still felt like something was wrong. That he should have told her.

He must have picked up on her discomfort, for he leaned up on one elbow so he was looking down at her.

"You have a problem with me and your brother hanging out?" "No. Of course not. It just feels strange that he doesn't know about us."

"Rose, no one knows about us, remember? You wanted it that way."

"Right. Of course, you're right."

"Unless you want to start changing the rules?"

She was startled by the question. Change the rules? She looked up into his eyes and saw that he wasn't joking. "Change the rules how?"

He shrugged. "They're your rules. We could start by letting your brother know we're spending some time together. Maybe take this outside once in a while."

"Maybe we could take it all the way to your house," she said, warming up to the idea.

He seemed less warm about the idea of her in his home. "You want to come to my place?" He sounded so horrified by the notion that she immediately nodded and said, "Yes, yes I do." And as she said the words she realized how true they were. She was dying to see Matt's home. To see how he lived. She was pretty sure he was a bit of a slob based on the general slovenliness of his appearance, but how bad of a slob was he? Did he have roommates? A pet of any kind? Pornographic art on the walls? Student furniture? For all she knew he'd hired a decorator and the inside of his home was a show place. She had no way of knowing since he'd never invited her over.

"How did me suggesting we let your brother know about us turn into you wanting to see inside my house?"

"I don't know, but I like that it did."

"Okay. You can come over."

"Great. When? Tomorrow?" Making a date for tomorrow was advance planning in their relationship.

He shook his head. "Not tomorrow. I have to clean up first. You can come Friday. I'll cook."

"You cook?"

"I cook."

"Okay, then. Friday it is." Then she nudged him. "We've already changed the rules."

"How so?"

"We've never planned that many days in advance before."

"Write it in your calendar so you don't forget."

"I won't forget."

Nineteen

ROSE TOOK A few minutes between patients to check her messages the next day. Nothing from Matt, but then she imagined he had quite a bit of cleaning up to do before he let her into his place the following day. She contemplated messaging him and inviting him to her place tonight. She knew from his schedule that he finished at five. How much cleaning up time could he need? Maybe she'd wait and if he didn't message her later she'd text him.

Her nurse came in between patients carrying a gorgeous bouquet of flowers. Roses, lilies, something yellow, and that ferny green stuff from the florist. "These just came for you," Deirdre said. "You sure made somebody happy."

She tried to imagine who'd sent her flowers. It wasn't her birthday, she hadn't delivered a baby, saved a life or done anything remarkable enough for a floral arrangement this incredible. It flashed through her mind that they might be from Matt and the thought died on the vine. Somehow, she didn't see Matt as the extravagant floral bouquet type.

"Wow." She took the small white envelope that was attached, opened it and quickly scanned the note on the card.

It was from Peter Buckingham. The note said, With Fond Regards. What on earth?

She then checked her emails. Flipped through routine messages, deleted some junk she'd never have time to read, and came upon an email that almost made her drop her phone.

Peter had also emailed her. The message read:

Dear Rose,

He was always a little formal.

I'm in Seattle for a few days and I thought I'd fly to Portland in the morning. Would you like to have lunch with me?

Always, Peter.

Her heart began to pound and she was taken back to those wonderful days when he'd wined and dined her, when they'd attended charity balls and she'd actually had a reason to buy some of the gowns she always loved but never had any place to wear.

She began to parse out the message like a high school girl with a note from a guy she likes. "I thought I'd fly down to Portland." What did that mean, exactly? He already had business here and would be in the area? They'd grab a burger or a sandwich and catch up like old friends? Or was he flying down especially to see her? But then why the short notice? Did he remember that she avoided patients on Friday afternoons so she could catch up on paperwork? Which she could as easily do over the weekend? And 'always' Peter. What did that mean? Always what? Love always? Peter will always be my name?

More to the point, should she go?

But from the moment she'd finished the email she knew she'd go. The biggest question in her mind was why he suddenly wanted to have lunch with her when they hadn't been in touch in almost a year, and, of course, what should she wear?

When Peter called her later in the day she was expecting it. After the initial greetings, he said, "I hope you can come to lunch tomorrow. Dreadful short notice, for which I apologize, but tomorrow's the only day I've got and I had to lie and make you an important client to get even that much time off." Well, at least she wasn't a last minute add-on to his schedule because something else had fallen through.

"No. It's fine. I'd love to have lunch with you. Do you want me to book something?"

"I took the liberty of booking a table. He named the most trendy and probably most expensive restaurant in Portland. She felt a flutter against her ankles, like the sway of a silk ball gown. "I like a man who thinks of everything."

"Wonderful. I'll see you there at one o'clock."

"I'll look forward to it."

And then she did nothing of the sort. She fussed and wondered, and re-read his note and tried to find meaning between the lines. Matt texted her around nine that night:

Exhausted from housework, but not too tired. You?

She texted back,

Catching up on paperwork. See you tomorrow

night.

It was true, she was catching up on paperwork, but that was because she was taking tomorrow afternoon off. She suffered a pang, a sharp sear of betrayal. But it was only lunch with an old friend. Wasn't it?

It's just lunch, Rose reminded herself as she changed her outfit for the third time. She was going for elegant but casual. She put away the Chanel suit. It was too Ladies who Lunch. She didn't know what had possessed her to buy the damn thing in the first place. In the end she wore a simple green sheath dress with a chunky gold necklace Peter had bought her and a pair of Prada heels. Not many men could appreciate a designer shoe. Peter Buckingham was one of those few.

She told herself it was only a casual lunch, though the sight of his flowers broadcast a different message.

She walked into the restaurant at precisely one and found Peter already arrived. He must have passed the hostess a photo of her or something for the young woman took one look at her and said, "Right this way, Sir Peter is waiting."

The second he spotted her he stood, stepped forward and kissed her discreetly. "Lovely to see you," he murmured, before they both sat at what had to be the best table in the house.

"Dropped your title again, I see," she said.

He was completely unrepentant. "Americans are so impressed by a title. Next to being a film star, it's the best way to get a good table."

"You are shameless."

"And you are as beautiful as I remember."

A bottle of champagne appeared. Dom, probably

vintage. "Are we celebrating?" she asked as the sommelier poured them each a glass of the golden, bubbling wine.

"Seeing you again is definitely cause for celebration."

He was exactly the same, she realized as they began to chat. Easily, because they'd always been easy around each other. He was still the slightly round-cheeked but very attractive man. Like a devilish cherub, she'd always thought. He was dressed, as was his habit on business, in a handmade Savile Row suit, this one a camel color. Like hers, his shoes were Prada.

He twinkled engagingly at her. "Tell me everything," he said.

No. No. She wasn't going to play that game. "Why did you send me flowers and invite me to lunch?"

He sighed and settled back in his chair. A waiter discretely placed plates of smoked salmon in front of them. The fish so thin you could see the plate beneath. When he'd withdrawn, Peter said, "It always takes me a day or two to adjust to how direct Americans are."

"Saves time and misunderstandings," she said, sticking a fork into her salmon.

"I ordered ahead. But if you prefer to peruse a menu, it's easily done."

"No. This is fine."

He remembered how much she liked smoked salmon. She bet this meal was going to be amazing.

"Why did I get hold of you again?" He put down his wine and leaned closer to her. "The simple truth is that I haven't been able to forget you."

Once more she felt that odd sensation, like a brush

of silk against her ankles, a dash of head spinning as though she were waltzing. "You didn't try very hard to keep me." Maybe that sounded as though she cared more than she wished to, or that he'd broken her heart. But she found she didn't want to be coy or play games any more than she wanted him to. She wanted to deal plainly, talk openly.

"Were you always this blunt?"

"Probably not." She'd fallen into the habit of speaking whatever she thought to Matt and knowing he spoke to her the same way.

"I regret not keeping in touch very much." He ate a bit of his salmon and so did she. Oh, and she might have had a small orgasm in her mouth from the burst of flavor. The salmon was served with some kind of fancy cream and, well, she had no idea what they'd done to the salmon but it was amazing. "This will sound arrogant, I suppose. But I want to be completely honest with you. I enjoyed our time together more than I realized at the time. I did want to continue, but the logistics were a nightmare. We live on different continents, in opposite time zones, you have a career, community, family here. As I do in England. How could I ask you to give all that up?"

It occurred to her that it would have been her decision to give those things up for him or not. But he hadn't given her the option. "I suppose it was easier to let things fizzle out."

Which they did pretty rapidly once he stopped putting any effort into the long-distance relationship. One phone call stuck in her mind. It was toward the end and she'd suggested they both take a week's vacation and meet somewhere. She'd suggested the Caribbean, not that it was exactly half way between them, but it would have been a sort of compromise. He'd waffled and finally said he couldn't find the time, but he'd sounded odd and she concluded he had another interest. "I got the feeling you were seeing someone else."

"Damn it, Rose. You see too much. It's absolutely uncanny."

"So you were dating someone."

"I was. A lovely woman in her way. And she lives in London which made things much easier." He paused and sighed, as though what he was about to say was bad news. "But she wasn't you. I don't know. You never make a scene, you don't ever ask the question a man dreads most, 'does this look good on me?'" She had to grin at his terrible falsetto impersonation of a woman having a wardrobe dilemma. "You say the right things, can converse on any subject. You're beautiful, desirable, and frankly, I was a fool to let you go."

The salmon had been succeeded by tiny portions of something on tiny squares of something else that seemed too pretty to eat. Besides, it was difficult to concentrate on food while her stomach was full of extremely acrobatic butterflies.

She might be an educated professional too old to be a romantic fool, but she'd literally dreamed of this moment. Sometimes, to her shame, she'd even been awake when she'd dreamed that Peter told her she was the most amazing woman in the world and he wanted her to be his forever.

Whoa there, Nellie, he hadn't said anything like that. Maybe all he wanted was to get her back into bed now that he was in the neighborhood. So, she said, "I think so too."

He chuckled. "I forgot to mention your sense of humor."

She had a moment, a flash of knowledge, where she absolutely knew he'd written a pro and con list about her.

"What are my negatives?" she asked, going with her instinct.

He appeared taken back by the question. "Your negatives?"

"Yes. Obviously you've given this a lot of thought. You've told me all the reasons why you're here, but what were the ones that kept you away?"

"Not kept me away, exactly. But there is the distance, of course. And your work is here, your life is here." He put up his hands, not like a fugitive surrendering to a cop, more like a card player showing his hand. "I was worried you wouldn't fit into my world. It's a set of rules and obligations one is born into."

"So, what do you want from me?"

"I realized that my mother and sisters can show you everything you need to know. And you're clever enough to pick up the rest on your own." He sipped at his wine—they'd had a different glass slipped in front of them to match each course. "I'm making a terrible mess of this. But, Rose, I'm asking you to marry me."

She'd been pleasantly doing a Cinderella waltz in her head without even realizing it, now the music came to a crashing halt and she stood there somewhere between the eleventh chime of the clock and the twelfth. In those seconds before the princess turns back into the servant girl dressed in rags.

"You're asking me to marry you?" She felt breathless, stunned.

"I'm sorry. I've never proposed before. I made a dreadful mess of it."

"No. I'm just surprised." Like she was having an out-of-body-experience surprised. Like a team of aliens had turned the corner and asked her directions to the White House surprised.

"If I had time, I'd have worked my way up to this, but I've got to get back to Seattle. We're working flat out. And then I'm on a plane back to London. But I do miss you terribly. Will you think about it?"

"Of course."

After that, they ploughed through about thirty-five more courses of delicious food that she barely tasted.

Now that his proposal had been delivered, Peter seemed to relax. He was funny, charming, sexy and rich. While she hadn't exactly warmed to his family, and suspected they felt the same, she did care for Peter.

But enough to marry him?

When lunch was over, he glanced at his watch and made a face. "I've got to get back. I've got a car picking me up in ten minutes to take me back to the airport."

"You seriously flew down here to take me to lunch?"

"Of course. I only wish I could stay longer. But look, come to London. Make whatever arrangements you need to at work, and come. I miss you."

She walked out with him, and a shiny black town car sat in front of the restaurant waiting for him. "Can I drop you somewhere?"

She shook her head. "Thank you for coming. Thank you for the flowers, and for lunch." Thank you for offering me that role of princess I've been auditioning for my whole life.

"It was my pleasure," he said with absolute sincerity. "Call me anytime, day or night."

Then he pulled her to him and kissed her. It was a daytime kiss, nothing too over the top, but her body remembered the taste of him and the feel of him. They hugged tightly and then he was climbing into the town car and waving to her through the window.

Twenty

WHEN SHE KNOCKED on Matt's door not many hours later, she still felt lightheaded from the shock of receiving her first marriage proposal. And not exactly one she'd been expecting, either.

Matt opened the door. He was clean-shaven but she could see he hadn't put a lot of effort into it. He didn't wear Savile Row. She thought he might be wearing Levis, but the football shirt hung over the belt line so she couldn't be sure. He looked good, though. And the house smelled so good her heart sank. She was still full from the ninety-five-course lunch.

He pulled her to him and kissed her, hard and hungry. For a second she felt stunned. Two men kissing her in one day?

He pulled back, a quizzical expression on his face. "Everything okay?"

"Yes. Sorry, I was distracted by the cooking smells. You really do cook."

"Sure do. I hope you're hungry."

She was so full she thought a sip of ice water might

do her in. "What is it? Smells amazing."

"Moussaka. It's a family recipe. Come in the kitchen and talk to me. It's almost ready."

As they walked through she checked out the main living area and glimpsed a fireplace with a beautiful carved mantel that looked original, hardwood floors that could use refinishing, a couple of art deco stained-glass windows. His furniture was solid, Mission-style pieces that were probably reproduction, but good ones. She was impressed. Of course, if she lived here, she'd do more with the art and accessories, and tidy up the built-in bookshelves.

The kitchen was a mix of old and new. He or someone had refinished the cabinets, some of which were glass-fronted, but the counters were granite and the appliances were modern and top-of-the-line.

"Gorgeous house," she said.

"Glad you like it."

He poured her a glass of wine and she sipped it. The atmosphere was strange between them and she knew it was coming from her.

He glanced up from chopping tomatoes. "Busy day?"

"A surprising one."

"Yeah? Somebody pop a baby without scheduling it first?"

"No. I had lunch with an old friend."

He paused the knife and gave her his full attention. "Yeah?"

"It was Peter Buckingham."

"The lord."

"The baronet. Yes."

He put down the chopping knife. His face, usually so full of expression, gave nothing away. "Did you have a good time?"

"Yes. He's always good company." She took another sip of wine. "Matt, he asked me to marry him." She waited, her breath suspended in her throat.

He picked up his beer and drank. Time ticked by with agonizing slowness. Then he said, "Well, we always knew this day would come. I didn't expect it this fast, but hey, good for you. It's what you've always wanted."

"I had no idea he was even in the country. I don't want you to think I was keeping anything from you." No! That wasn't what she meant to say. She was so confused. She wanted to share a truly astonishing piece of news with the person she most wanted to share everything with.

"We've been clear about you and me from the start. It was great while it lasted. No hard feelings. I'll miss the sex, but I wish you well."

"That's it?"

"What more do you want?" his voice was slightly sarcastic.

"I thought—" Oh, God, she'd been such a fool. She'd set the rules, she'd been the one going on and on about boundaries and then she'd completely screwed it all up. She'd gone and fallen in love with Matt. She hadn't even realized until Peter proposed, and, as he'd driven away, she'd known she could never be Lady Buckingham. Because she was deeply and hopelessly in love with Matt.

Maybe she still wasn't through with fairy tales.

She'd wanted Matt to fight for her, to beg her not to marry Peter. To ask her to marry him.

But, instead of fighting to keep her in his life, he was pretty much booting her out of it.

"I don't think I'll stay for dinner after all." Because she suddenly felt that she couldn't be cool and pretend to eat and pretend everything was okay. Because it wasn't okay.

"Suit yourself," he said, as though he couldn't care less and there were a dozen other women waiting on speed dial who'd be only too happy to chow down on his home-cooked Greek food.

She got through her week, blessing her patients for keeping her too busy to brood. Almost. Friday, she packed up her laptop and a weekend bag, got into her car and drove to Hidden Falls. She wanted to check on her dad, but also, she wanted to be with people who loved her unconditionally.

When she got home, she learned that Jack had found a physician only twenty minutes drive away. This was good. She obviously didn't put up with any crap, and he respected that. Also good.

She could see his color was better and he'd happily given up the idea of planting artichokes when Marguerite came up with the idea of growing more heirloom varieties, not only of tomatoes, which everyone was doing, but also squashes, peas, beans. He was happily researching heirloom plants and testing out the best places to plant them.

"I have to hand it to you," Rose said to Marguerite as they sat over green tea on her porch. They'd let the hens out of their enclosure and they were happily pecking and preening. One was giving itself a dust bath in the flower bed outside Marguerite's cottage. "You got Dad engaged in something that interests him and doesn't tire him out. Or wreck anything."

"It wasn't easy. I got the idea from something Alexei said."

Rose turned to stare. "Alexei? You mean Matt's brother?"

"Yes. We've been emailing. I think he might take a trip here one day soon. He really likes the idea of sourcing as much produce locally as he can. I've got the full network of contacts."

Rose wondered if Alexei's interest was purely agricultural, but kept her mouth shut since she was the last person who understood male/female relationships.

Marguerite poured more tea from an authentic Japanese teapot and asked, "Whatever happened with you and Matt? Mom was convinced there was something going on there."

She shrugged, holding her emotions in check with an effort.

"It's a casual thing." So casual that he'd pretty much ended it without a fight, and hadn't bothered to contact her all week. She took a sip of tea to ease her throat.

Marguerite shook her head. "You know how people say to women sometimes, 'you date like a guy, or you have sex like a guy,' like that's somehow a good thing?"

"Yeah. I guess."

"Well, you're doing it. And I don't think it's a good thing."

"Why? Why not? What is wrong with a relationship

that has all the good things and none of the bad? I can enjoy the sex, the fun flirty texts, without having to go to sporting events I hate, or meet people I have no interest in. I don't have to sit through movies I don't want to see because it's his turn to pick. I'm too busy for that. And so is Matt. Why are you so hostile to the idea?"

"Because that's not a relationship. It's a bed buddy."

She almost laughed except that she was too irritated to laugh. "A bed buddy? That sounds like something you'd call pest control for."

"You know what I mean." Marguerite primmed her mouth. "I've decided to give up swearing. Well, I'm trying to anyway."

"Why?"

"I read an article or maybe heard something on NPR that suggested when you swear you're just being lazy. Using real language is better."

"And all of this freed up brain power gave you bed buddy?"

How could you stay mad at someone who so earnestly tried to improve herself, her soil, her food, the planet. Rose was a bit fuzzy on what being a flower child actually meant, she thought it might be because the hippies used to carry flowers and pass them out to soldiers and passers by. Marguerite seemed like a flower child in that she lived in her enchanted garden, her biggest enemies were slugs, and even those she tried to deter or reroute rather than kill.

Marguerite put her hands on her hips. "I'm a work in progress here, most of the day I talk to plants and chickens."

And because Marguerite was one of the nicest people Rose knew, and because she was hurting, she let down her guard and told the truth. "You're right. It didn't work at all. I tried so hard to keep things casual, but I fell in love with Matt. And he dumped me." There. She'd said it. The awful truth that made the idea of ever going back to Pacific Crest hospital a nightmare to be dreaded. She'd set the rules up herself, and then she'd broken all of them.

Her sister smiled, looking thrilled. "You love him."

"And he dumped me."

Marguerite looked puzzled. "Why would he dump you for being in love with him? Isn't that a good thing?"

"I've never, ever told a man I love him so I think I did it all wrong."

"It's three words. How could you screw it up?" Her sister wasn't being sarcastic. She looked truly confused.

"Because I had lunch with Peter Buckingham that same day, and Peter asked me to marry him. When I told Matt about the proposal, he just blew me off, like I meant nothing to him."

"Peter Buckingham proposed?"

"Yes."

"And you turned him down?"

"Yes."

"Oh, I'm so glad." A black and white cat Rose didn't recognize jumped onto the porch, stalked past her and jumped into Marguerite's lap. The cat glared through narrowed green eyes at the chickens, but didn't attempt to bother them. As Marguerite stroked the cat, she said, "What about when you told him you love him?"

"I didn't. In my head, he was going to say, 'Don't marry Peter. Marry me!' And we'd have that perfect moment where you both admit you're crazy about each other. Instead he said, 'No problem, It's been fun. See you around.'"

Marguerite looked as sad as she did when one of their hens died of old age. "And Peter Buckingham?"

"I considered his proposal for about ten minutes, then called him on his way to the airport and politely declined."

"So, if Peter hadn't proposed, maybe you wouldn't have discovered you love Matt."

"Maybe. So?"

She spread her hands, her silver rings sparkling. "So, maybe he needs time to realize he loves you."

"If he loved me, he'd have tried to keep me in his life. He ended things like he didn't care at all."

"Rose, I saw the way he looked at you. That is not a man who doesn't care at all."

She rubbed her forehead where a headache was starting. "So, what do I do?"

"Go and tell him how you feel."

She was not in love with this plan. "But if he doesn't feel anything for me, I'll humiliate myself."

"Isn't a little humiliation better than a lifetime of regret?"

"I'll get back to you on that."

Twenty-One

MATT WASN'T ONE to wear his heart on his sleeve. He always had something going on. He was a busy man with lives to save, baskets to shoot, a lawn to mow.

But he couldn't stop the dull ache that had settled in his chest after Rose announced she was marrying her English prince.

When James called and asked him to go shooting, he jumped at the opportunity.

They went to the law enforcement range, and got set up.

Matt hadn't planned to say anything, but suddenly, over the muffled shots of other gunmen practicing and the thuds as bullets hit the dirt behind the targets, he blurted, "I'm in love with your sister."

James took time to set up his shot. "Thought you might be." He squeezed the trigger slowly and killed the paper zombie.

"What are you, psychic? I've never said a thing."

"I know. After Harvey's wedding, you both stopped mentioning the other one's name. Dead giveaway."

"Well, there's one big problem. She's marrying that English dick."

James closed one eye, breathed in as he'd taught them the night of the stag, held his breath and squeezed the trigger. "Yes! Straight in the heart." Then he turned to Matt. "No, she's not marrying the English dick. She turned him down."

Matt felt like he'd been shot straight in the heart. He narrowed his gaze. "Don't mess with me."

"I'm not. Sir Peter asked her to be Lady Buckingham and she said, 'No, thank you.'"

"How do you know?"

"Because she told me."

He was having trouble taking this in. "Why didn't she tell me?"

"I don't know. Maybe you didn't ask? Look, she's my sister and you're my friend. I do not want to get in the middle of anything." He turned back to his weapon. "You want to know more, go ask her yourself."

James was right. She'd told him Peter Buckingham had proposed, but he'd never asked her how she'd answered.

He was so completely in love with that woman, had been from the start, and she'd always been cool, aloof. She'd insisted on casual, and he'd agreed because he thought casual was better than nothing. But had her feelings changed? Was it possible?

One thing was certain, he was going to ask her to her face. Maybe let her know how he felt. Even if she rejected him, he couldn't feel worse than he already had this past week.

"Thanks. Mind if I cut out early? Think I'll run over

to her place now."

"She won't be home. She's in Hidden Falls for the weekend." James clicked on the safety and put down his weapon. "I'll give you the address."

Rose was peeling a mound of potatoes, Daphne was chopping carrots, and Marguerite was setting the big table in the dining room. "How many am I laying for, Mom?"

"Let's see, we three, your father, Iris and Geoff are coming, oh, and put out dessert forks. Iris is bringing one of her famous pies from her bakery. James said he'd probably come by. How many is that?"

"Seven."

"Good. I'm cooking for ten, so if neighbors or more family show up we have enough. If not, we'll have leftovers tomorrow."

Rose didn't know how her mom did it, but she always had enough food. If twenty people showed up, she'd pick a few more things from the garden, open up her big freezer and dig out a premade casserole. No one would go home hungry.

"What are we having?"

"Beef stew, and vegetable stew for the vegetarians."

Through the open kitchen window, she could hear the sound of a vehicle driving up. Lucky, their retriever, lifted her head and then rose to her feet and headed for the door, barking, which meant she didn't recognize the visitor.

Daphne dried her hands and was already walking to the front door when the doorbell rang.

Rose peeked out the window, and her heart began to stutter. She knew that truck.

Sure enough, in much less time than she needed to prepare herself to see Matt, he was inside the house, talking to her mom, asking after Jack.

Marguerite nudged her. "Go on, go talk to him."

She wiped her own hands, pulled in a breath and walked out to find Matt patting Lucky. He looked like he'd been gardening, or cleaning out the garage or something. He had dust on his jeans and an old plaid shirt on.

She didn't care. She wanted to throw herself in his arms, dust and all. Instead, she said, "Matt. What a surprise."

When he glanced at her she felt a week of misery intensify into one painful stab. How could he not love her? How could he not see how much she loved him?

He didn't look like he'd been getting a lot of sleep, but that probably only meant he'd been on call all week.

He straightened. "Rose, would you like to take a walk?"

"Um, sure. Let me grab my shoes."

She was so flustered she couldn't remember where she'd left her shoes, or what shoes she'd been wearing, so she stuffed her feet into purple plastic Crocs that she thought might belong to her mother. He opened the front door and she followed him out. "This is a gorgeous property," he said.

"We like it. I'll take you out by the pond, there's a nice walking trail."

Vigorous scratching could be heard on the door behind them and she realized that Lucky was not in a mood to be tactful. "Mind if the dog comes?"

He shook his head. "No."

She opened the door and Lucky bounded out, looking like she'd been let out of prison. She frisked, and bounded, found one of her million tennis balls and picked it up, threw it in the air, and then dropped it at Matt's feet.

"She's flirting with you," Rose told him.

"Glad someone is," he replied, then bent, picked up the ball and hurled it. Lucky took off at a gallop.

She ignored the comment, but her heart was thudding.

"Your mom says your dad's doing really well."

"He is." She led him down the path. Ahead of them, the dog had found the ball, or maybe another ball which would be good enough for her, and was already turning to head back toward them. "Did you come to check on my dad?"

He turned. "No. I came to check on you. There are some things I want to say." He stepped closer, and a yellow ball thwacked his foot, accompanied by a canine whine. He glanced down. "Lucky, you are really cramping my style here." The dog grinned and wagged her tail and once more Matt threw the ball, this time putting every bit of muscle into it so the dog had a lot farther to go.

He turned back. He looked so good. She didn't care that he needed a shave or that the best use of that shirt would be to buff furniture.

"I need to ask you something, something I should have asked a week ago. Are you planning to marry Peter Buckingham?"

"No."

His eyes closed briefly. "I am such an idiot."

"Yes. But so was I. I should have told you. I thought you'd ask. I wanted you to." She shook her head. "No, the truth is, I wanted you to fight for me."

"But you'd gone on about him and it was obvious that you regretted the end of the relationship. I figured he was everything you wanted."

"A year ago, I'd have agreed with you." She'd had some time to think this through. She glanced around at the green, leafy trees and the pond where Lucky was wading for the ball. "I never thought I belonged here. I believed all the fairy tales. I was that princess dropped in the wrong family. And when Peter came along, I felt like he was there to claim me, to take me to the world where I did belong. When he proposed I had a moment. A total fantasy, fairy-tale ending moment. But when you close the book, or the movie ends, the fantasy's over and you go back to real life.

"Peter was a fantasy for me. I never loved him. I loved the idea of him. When I thought about marrying him, all I could think about was how much I couldn't lose you." She gazed into his eyes, and saw deep understanding there. "Because you are my reality."

He seemed pretty happy with her answer. She waited for him to kiss her, for everything to go back to normal, but he said, "I don't want to push things here, but is there any chance you might one day love me?"

She laughed, a slightly hysterical sound. "That's what I'm saying. I do love you."

"That is very good news, because I love you, too."

He pulled her into his arms and kissed her and she felt how solid he was. How real.

She pulled away. "I thought you were maybe too

scarred to love again, after you fell for that woman and she didn't love you back."

He laughed, low and sexy. "That woman was you."

Her mouth fell open in shock. "Me?"

"Sure. I thought you guessed. I've been in love with you probably since the first moment I saw you."

"No! Not love at first sight?"

"Sucks, doesn't it?"

"But we're scientists, we don't believe in–"

"Magic? I think maybe I do."

He kissed her again, and she thought maybe she believed in magic, too.

Other Books you Might Enjoy

The best way to keep up with new releases, plus enjoy bonus content and prizes is to join Nancy's newsletter at nancywarren.net.

The Almost Wives Club

One possibly cursed wedding gown and five runaway brides.

The Almost Wives Club: Kate, Book One
Secondhand Bride, Book Two
Bridesmaid for Hire, Book Three
The Wedding Flight, Book Four
If the Dress Fits, Book Five

The Take a Chance Series

Meet the chance family, a cobbled together family of eleven kids who are all grown up and finding their ways in life and love.

Chance Encounter, Prequel
Kiss a Girl in the Rain, Book One
Iris in Bloom Take a Chance, Book Two
Blueprint for a Kiss Take a Chance, Book Three
Love to Go Take a Chance, Book Five

Toni Diamond Mysteries

Toni is a successful saleswoman for Lady Bianca Cosmetics in this series of humorous cozy mysteries. Along with having an eye for beauty and a head for business, Toni's got a nose for trouble and she's never shy about following her instincts, even when they lead to murder.

Frosted Shadow, Book One
Ultimate Concealer, Book Two
Midnight Shimmer, Book Three

For a complete list of books, check out Nancy's website at nancywarren.net.

About the Author

Nancy Warren is the *USA Today* bestselling author of more than sixty novels. She's known for writing funny, sexy and suspenseful tales. She calls Vancouver, Canada home though she tends to wander. She's an avid hiker, animal lover, wine drinker and chocolate fiend. Favorite moments in her career include being featured on the front page of the New York Times when she launched Harlequin's NASCAR series with Speed Dating. She was also the answer to a crossword puzzle clue in Canada's National Post newspaper. She's a finalist for the 2015 Rita awards for Blueprint for a Kiss, the third book in the Take a Chance series, and has won the Reviewer's Choice Award from Romantic Times magazine among other awards. She spills secrets in her newsletter and you can sign up at www.nancywarren.net or come visit her on Facebook at www.facebook.com/nancy.warren.9655 and on Twitter @nancywarren1.